TENDER GIRL

A NOVEL

ALSO BY LISA SAMUELS

ANTI M (CHAX PRESS 2013)

WILD DIALECTICS (SHEARSMAN BOOKS 2012)

TOMORROWLAND CDS (VOICE & INSTRUMENTALS)
(DEEP SURFACE 2012)

GENDER CITY (SHEARSMAN BOOKS 2011)

MAMA MORTALITY CORRIDOS (HOLLOWAY PRESS 2010)

TOMORROWLAND (SHEARSMAN BOOKS 2009)

THROE (OYSTERCATCHER PRESS 2009)

THE INVENTION OF CULTURE (SHEARSMAN BOOKS 2008)

INCREMENT (A FAMILY ROMANCE) (BRONZE SKULL PRESS 2006)

PARADISE FOR EVERYONE (SHEARSMAN BOOKS 2005)

WAR HOLDINGS (PAVEMENT SAW PRESS 2003)

ANARCHISM IS NOT ENOUGH BY LAURA RIDING (CRITICAL
EDITION) (UNIVERSITY OF CALIFORNIA PRESS 2001)

THE SEVEN VOICES (O BOOKS 1998)

POETRY AND THE PROBLEM OF BEAUTY (EDITOR) (MODERN
LANGUAGE STUDIES 1997)

LETTERS (MEOW PRESS 1996)

TENDER GIRL

by

LISA SAMUELS

DUSIE

Grateful acknowledgement is made to the editors of the journals in which pieces of this book first appeared: *Brief, Chicago Review, Hotel Amerika, Text*.

Cover image: treated sculpture by Debra Bernier
Author photo by Tim Page

Layout and design by Lisa Samuels and DUSIE
Kingston, Rhode Island

First printing, Lisa Samuels 2015

ISBN-13: 9780981980898

This book is for women who help me imagine,
and who can imagine it

CONTENTS

Se trouvent en présence le nageur et la femelle de requin, sauvée par lui.
Ils se regardèrent entre les yeux pendant quelques minutes; et chacun
s'étonna de trouver tant de férocité dans les regards de l'autre. Ils tournent
en rond en nageant, ne se perdent pas de vue, et se disent à part soi: «Je
me suis trompé jusqu'ici; en voilà un qui est plus méchant.» Alors, d'un
commun accord, entre deux eaux, ils glissèrent l'un vers l'autre, avec une
admiration mutuelle, la femelle de requin écartant l'eau de ses nageoires,
Maldoror battant l'onde avec ses bras: et retinrent leur souffle, dans une
vénération profonde, chacun désireux de contempler, pour la première fois,
son portrait vivant. Arrivés à trois mètres de distance, sans faire aucun
effort, ils tombèrent brusquement l'un contre l'autre, comme deux aimants,
et s'embrassèrent avec dignité et reconnaissance, dans une étreinte aussi
tendre que celle d'un frère ou d'une sœur. Les désirs charnels suivirent
de près cette démonstration d'amitié. Deux cuisses nerveuses se collèrent
étroitement à la peau visqueuse du monstre, comme deux sangsues; et,
les bras et les nageoires entrelacés autour du corps de l'objet aimé qu'ils
entouraient avec amour, tandis que leurs gorges et leurs poitrines ne
faisaient bientôt plus qu'une masse glauque aux exhalaisons de goëmon;
au milieu de la tempête qui continuait de sévir; à la lueur des éclairs;
ayant pour lit d'hyménée la vague écumeuse, emportés par un courant
sous-marin comme dans un berceau, et roulant, sur eux-mêmes, vers les
profondeurs inconnues de l'abîme, ils se réunirent dans un accouplement
long, chaste et hideux!... Enfin, je venais de trouver quelqu'un qui me
ressemblât!... Désormais, je n'étais plus seul dans la vie!... Elle avait les
mêmes idées que moi!... J'étais en face de mon premier amour!

Comte de Lautréamont (Isidore Ducasse), *Les Chants de Maldoror* (1868)

PRELUDE

TIRADE

Really love, you construe with optimal tongue motion the words you
have said inside your mind and now re-formulate, as though love were a
thought et al. Dewish with pardon, we slip our arms together and make
a pact to pearled clemency. Gentle gentle.

HAZARD

The girl appears all limbs and sheen, cars swerve, the clouds sift down
over the city suturing this to that for tender. Girl opened her eyes for
the first time to the flesh of her mother. Strudels. Donuts. Pies. Tender
seaweed. Salt licks on the soft grasses by the little holes for breathing.
The wet veil pushes, splits, Girl looks around: the salt swerves spin to
vortices, vortices into mouths, thick spit all round the eyes. She flicks
herself out quickly mouth upturned, the flash the streaming holes out
swirling. *Hhhhh.* Hhhh.

They go raspy and gargantuan at once, wholistic curving bodies turning
delicate in the waves. The open water moves the light and dark, your
body growing the elliptical voyage and eating, eating, cold hot swirls in
the mouth. Meshing young rubbed visitors and looping cycles of deep
and up, swim and return.

[THE STORY OPENS – GIRL IS OCEAN BORN AND LIVES]

11

Then there's the land of the father, let's go see. The undeclared beach and seafoam roll her in, hhhh, the little holes for breathing give their weather up gentle.

AT SEA

The men perambulating through coastal elocutions, all the same waste we put out hands for she arrived and we were duty-bound to caress, to bridge over impediments, to sing in our cracky voices some tunes we'd remembered from culture, weeded the swing-set and put her in it, the vines creeping up the windows in a friendly fashion, doll house grown bigger, the ship having been distended for so many years we'd brought on heaps of earth by now, the trees grew nicely yellow and orange and red promises around the bow, the plastic platypuses keeping them company and startling the seabirds who rested sometimes near the croaky chairs we sat her in, offering a story, singing our songs by way of payment to the circular logic that steered our ship ashore. What a fine one what a find.

TENDERIZE

She was a vegetable made of parts, not meat at all. She was a fish made of body parts. She was a wet tree mostly underground when he walked along the way, the edges of the vaporous sea unaware of itself as needing any parts to play, though singing. "Hello, can you walk."
The full energy of the piece was dominant, partial in and out, the little holes for breathing let respire, *hhhhh*. The cartilage could hold you tenderly wrapped in hidden fat, never gaunt though lithe plump skeletal, tendons pulse. The sand's paved over, she's landed near the city edge. What's going to happen to Girl?

[GIRL GOES TO SHORE. SHIP-GOERS BRING HER ABOARD. A BEACH WALKER SPEAKS]

SHARK FIN SOUP
The market was full of the sliced-off crowns of her friends. They were salty and spicy, tangy and sweet past indigence. They could say nothing despite the abrasive little air holes they all bore. She breathed in and out and thus their stories were saturated with the resistance of non-industry.

While the man looked the other way she took the wax-paper tray in stealth, folded it, and made the thick surface smooth and pliant as never before, vivified. Girl covered them *in time* – the fish paper was angled, the angles were electric memes, ghazals staring from the dark. Mother mother, wet patchwork in the dark.

PLACE NAMES
Girl was begging this time, but softly, so as not to disturb the little holes for breathing through the dense air full of color. Smiling, they say thank you. Sweet like lachrymose roses striated next to the wavy yellow armature where she sat comparing under water with the surface aliens she leaned to. The air full of particles tinily fractured crash against her skin.

Delicious fishes in her mouth, the crunching armature the face bones chewing gently. Where she was *from* you wouldn't necessarily feel the blue-brown skin nor comply, you're simply there? The birds again as though like fish they got near – swift but never so much as a warning, dulcet falling rising side-by-side, lights in the daytime darkness. The wax paper held by her side, she was come to stay, convincing without words.

[GIRL CANNOT SPEAK. SHE IS HUNGRY; IN A MARKET SOMEONE GIVES HER FISH]

ONE
[THE PRINCE]

MOUTH

Her teeth were coated with days of food and later Girl would miss that, piles of discarded clothing all around the ground and no one ever to check. Chemicals and water and crystalline impressions on the patterned skin. Tweak tweak *hhhh*. Turn around and around, *the sun's eye is upon me* and the showers by the beaches are so cold they hurt her skin. She opens her mouth wide to cover up the sun.

CLAIMANT

You can fall in with someone, it's a kind of currency *you go one way with one body, another with another*, rise and fall. Deciduous trees rising and falling while the leaves fur in the wet air by the sea.
She can still feel the buzz near her, in her limbs where she could *feel* the saying hello of one person, of another immensely vertical and the sshhh, zzzzmmmm, husha in the land. "Such versatile enclosures," walk walk, walk walk, "what a beauty for curl" someone says with meat, pretty skin shuck rolled around delicious holes bat bat.

On a particular afternoon some trees lit themselves continuously before evening unfolded, so many bodies moving vertical and horizontal at once, their shafts truck through their ardor with appeal. Some bodies are smiling.

[LAND AND SKY STIMULI. GIRL IS YOUNG AND MEN BECKON]

Girl moves visible, her wet eyes shaking: at first he seemed headed another direction, *but once more he came softly after us,* curving around the building, beckoning. The arms and voices reached back and forth to begin what could henceforth be – a doping scene, an opening of body openings, a perking of the mind toward questions she could not get hold of yet, like "would you like a drink or a trip to paradise"?

Without answering him her eyes rolled all the way to his apartment. The ceiling arched up away from her, her cartilage null and braced, flushed, holding, separating. Liquidity's vast erasure rushed right to her and all over the pads holding the floor. Sounds too: the room was full of receding electronica that peeled the skin where the voice opened where you gripped it and the husk flies out the disks, speakers, hands of surprise – the room is full of savory water, dense with smelly luster, whoops!

TWONESS
She moved in where this beachy creature hovered loose and seasonal. This is a place to start.

Between the pillars were stairs, it was a large vase house designed like beasty life were flowers, set in a floating section of town up a hill. There were interior domicile walls Girl ran her hands on, regular spacing in between the box domains. Under the wooden air, there's "architecture" or architectonics. On the shelves tremendous objects stood quite still.

"Once or twice, and were you?" *Are you?*

We *told stories* licking salt and skin and Girl suddenly remembered the foamy tendril hair she came with. She had left it somewhere?, separating from her arms, left it slung over the turnstile where the pickets were

[GIRL GOES HOME WITH A MAN AND TAKES HIS SEXUAL LIFE. SHE MOVES IN WITH SOMEONE]

going forward by the pavement, near that market near the sea. The gates were how to get there.

He was transfixed by her minimal murmurs, moving her arms, her head's armature this way and that. He said she had a malady, something obsolescent streaming her response. *Hhhhhh*. She moved her head fast trying to catch up.

SOLUTION

Looking down Girl tried to heal her breaking skin under the sun of the apartment ledge. Afternoon. The blankets crumpled in damp hiding heaps, the sounds of dogs nearby. She peeled off pieces of her skin and left them there, strips of cotton soaking in salt water, soothing her. The blankets and skin resembled the heads of dogs.

The pale walls were shining at night as Girl formed movements in the buoyant air. She turns her bones gently back and forth, displace displace, the segregated legs move quietly.
Leaving the apartment she moved her body from *the boundary of terrain I am allowed, the steps and postures of categorical immanence, showing you believe in watery life.* Rubbing the orange across the bottoms of her feet then pushing against it smashing it. Epiform, she might know that, *come closer,* and this laterally moving body dangling out from her vertical torso perceptibly dripping holes.

The seasonal darkness and night sounds glow a greater distance this far from the sea-not-sea. *Air sounds, slightly crazed, ambulatory, but why not?* She walked, the floating air saturated with yeasts, particulates, oil droplets and dense perfumes, sniff sniff, Girl kept on moving, then sniff salt crystals, spiracles, held-back rain, open pores steaming. She followed her open face to the back yard of a house where the inhabitants were up late

[GIRL'S HAIR AND SKIN SLOUGH IN THE CHANGE FROM SEA TO LAND. THE MAN
WANTS TO SOLVE HER]

talking full of presence, their faces wobbling with talk, continuity and disruption on the same eyes in cartilaginous figurines clunking back and forth, their heads bobbing and strewing. *Ummer strew and wishal dreaming – bob and strew, yes yes, ha ha, I hit a world and you were in it dreaming of me and then I blank appeared.* See you say it like *that,* put that together with the dense faces. It was dark at the outer circle of the house light where Girl stood.

Later, in a stony part of the city, the mazes yielded for a while.
I mean segregating and re-grouping Girl moved in relation with her tribute to the land of the father, she was learning how to walk.
A man with a warm face beckoned her in. It was midnight and she held a cup in her hands and listened to the immigrant deliver his privilege. His warm hair was full of intention. He held her by the stomach and the rooms were square with wobbly walls, the fluid and colors came out, the hard-to-access insides a feature of the lateral surfaces of flesh squirming, the turns and slate eyes and the bathroom all had logics he would gesture. All the separate parts flung out.

Then his friends came over, wearing his robes and shining. *And how thrilling that moment,* the plates licked "make sure to get her home," and the sermonette discarded, the little holes for breathing armed.

Hhhh. It was a tall monument so why not leave the smashed glass?
It couldn't just rise up into the air, couldn't float or current. So walking was like that, glass underfoot.
The top of the air was pearling. *Her skin like glass suffused with wet, I am waiting to feel that, carved through with the wet glass, shivering.*

[GIRL WALKS AT NIGHT, SMELLING HUMAN TALK. A MAN PULLS HER IN]

LAY BY
When she opened her face several days on, the white car perched near
them with its gear. Across the valley, one tall mud-type building and
many smudge ones flat the mirror image of a city that wasn't decided.
Buildings hills and clouds.
Where were the places to get things? The places where people decided?
It was dry cramming for food and the outlines of the horizontal pieces
against each other moved slowly as Girl swiveled her face to each
opening entering her head: glue – petroleum – fur
– pheromones – nitrates – tiny seeds – bird-fluid
casting fine airsweat, swirls. The animosity of the human to airfluent
swirls, that pearly shine wet through the holes in the head, you open
your mouth to the taut pink and blue lines meeting the sky.
He breathed out huff. She got up from lying on the ground.

The man walking near her picked up shells. The first shot went low, like
a fake high-pitch thunder in the model of a city, "was that?" another one
a bit higher one direction or the other slightly left or slightly right of
where they walked. Girl and the man stepped half together he said "stop"
and walked her sideways, the body toward the car a damp machine.
They got back in.

Her seat in the car was not a replete place, it was crackly and exact, but
the discretion of the material made her breathless, smells emanating from
the factory where they did the machine-stitched composite. Girl held
her hands by her legs near her shell inside breathing *hhhh*. "Look here,"
there was a shell right-whorled where he held it in his hand. Round and
back and over, the displaced center of the act found its jarred familiar
breathing where you couldn't see. *Where* things were taking place, honey.

[THERE'S A CAR WITH THE DOMESTIC MAN. A GUNSHOT FROM AFAR]

"They do that around here." *Like "that's okay" like* what's coming toward me in electric water is a mild eyestorm in the glowish sea, *ssh hmm ahhhm*, a friendly roundabout with whorls puck pocked. The broken string of held living kite sounds, his voice, her voice muffled; she doesn't really talk yet she doesn't really yet know how.

TRAPEZE

The magenta prefix had arrived at last, the one from the market yum yum. The bed was on the floor and other furnishings were yet to come. His body rose like a telephone and ceased, Girl meanwhile pinpricking connections that stayed near waiting for something, a sign of their promised continuity, more *where you were* than *on the way* these walking penises liked language. She went long distances with her legs, placing them in dubious positions over dubious ground by walls: extending out particulates to feel.

One day she gathered messages with her fingers, *like in the movies*, one scrap of paper by the grass walk, picking her way looking, here's some "salt for your skin" messages creased in paper gathered bits on cardboard, tiny chemicals eating it, pieces on the walls by shops she flicks her fingers on. Her wanders lift her separateness deep into the beckoning of this life. She's separating one figure from the next, considering where something begins or ends.

Girl wondered about her new friend or the definition of leaving, a "mysterious and alluring" real being found traces like that bullet on that air near the car: a cruelty to learn, *hhhh*, walking toward and away from loose divergences of road, grass, gravel, walk, concrete, copper sky, not that she knew what it meant for anything to be "authentic" or otherwise. She tested on the lead of her mouth where things were *coming from*; she spit this dubious language practically.

[GIRL WORKS TO RECOGNIZE PATTERN, EXCURSION, TALK]

AFTER THE MANIFESTO
His range of books was heavy tide. Gathering up.
I've mistaken him for the genuine article: this prince is a little dim of lance balance, an antic busking circumference, explanations for innuendos, etc., over here the monkey leaping up to the heavy balloon in a past never to be repeated except in its exteriorization by the glamorous mind, a ballroom of staccato told to minsters who having heaved in the central chair were wooden ever after.

She did the language thing with images, flaring matchsticks one by one. Think about it carefully: the slivers of seaweed bought from the delicate store, one piece of translucent paper one open mouth. The delicate wetting inside her dark closed mouth. What animal turns to language? What animal turns to sound at all? How's sound image act? *I mean slowly "waking up" to fetish principles.*

In her hands the flares make near the holes one *word*, the man looking to see the holes, tender fingering, each one has entire faces in it smelling outward gulping in. In this set sound and light opens a series of rationales slowly holding the immediate world together and at a point, a light streaming live from ascent over the object monument in filaments. Scattered lucent stringlets hover. The rationale seemed to be a current fix, the heroine a copper wheel turning via citizens and exceptions or expectations; he read to her holding the books together the skin being live electric streaming beautiful smells. His range of books stands in for a composite "him."

SHE SAID BETWEEN YES AND NO
She pushed her fingers into the holes in her body: the anus the vagina the ears, the eyes the nose the mouth, wet and tender, pushing against the tiny holes the pores, these openings taut *would they go all the way through* completely traveling – no medial continuity for this wet body dripping in air, mother, breathe, turning *hhhhh.*

[HE READS TO HER. THE MOUTH EATS TALK AND LANGUAGE SALIVATES]

The next day a "strenuous conversation" like a vigil, a management council with the man who wanted stuff, his plans hijacked against a back wall of "character" or "rue" – a back bent back for whack and "parcel delivery" that's more like it he said when he was a child but getting over that, he stands up straighter now and knows how to "have" a conversation – *or can you manage a stable character for fuck's sake* – the words sashaying back and forth while she looked at him conscripted to the reveille as she had never planned.

Girl had no plan. The trees stood round admonishing. Pine, hackle, thrush. The boards had given all their pluck and were flat, silent, immured. Her mouth made those words, no no, no prince, price, pleased.

On the road
In the next town, the gatekeeper was an old man who looked down. He opened the gate readily when she came, and later some time pounded on the windows. You could get in anywhere young and sourceless, a bearded one smiling with his vegetables. In a garden room Girl was in his shirt with plates of green leaves circling around the kitchen. She had fallen by the door, he had "fallen on the chambermaid" like he said she would eat the green leaves up, they shucked and tinkled like open plates; a visitor arrived and walked all the way into the hall and she stood still as pillars pretending she weren't there.

Perhaps that's in another context, he archly observed, flexing his general knowledge muscles: of all the people, he smiled, her name is the most copious to me. Three plates later, she was walking through places like a three-dimensional film screen and these human projectors syntaxing their pulses, opening the holes in their faces and creasing to chew. My wouldn't you. The first man split his beard grinning *would you like to borrow my pajamas?* That was a sentence she practiced when she got wet.

[The domestic man propels identity. Girl leaves that seaside town]

Morning

The birds chitted in the trees and leaves against the panes of blue.
The sky sharp and the blasting outside went on as before but she held
her stomach with her hands to keep from resting. *An opportunity, a sincere
advantage* rapping her tangential. What to do?
To recognize the shapes of an "offer" on one side and a telling wound
on the other, an importunate person absorbing you in quasi-cinematic
desire-scopes. Hello seems not a question, not a going out at all; it is an
ask, "love" is a request. Which was this body.

Girl filled the chair like a hunting bag made from dense skin, she felt
gentle encouragement in the fibers of the wood. She licked at them
and pressed her eyeball between the curving slots of the chair. It
pushed back, Girl pressed the hard resistance of the fibers, she felt the
suppressed murmur of her blood. The wood pushed into her microscopic
barnacles, it was willing without being what a purpose might entail;
the wood arrayed the floaters brandishing air its own rights, it spiraled
out. To push enough you would reach the other side the fluid of the tree.
*I mean you'd go back to the sweat that made the tree and re-shaped it to another
purpose sitting there* the fingers of her hands, the water of her head, her
thick skin propelled.

I told you so

Girl is a true regarder, slack in the troth but fulsome in particulars, the
pulchritude he lusted for understood by her erroneously as pure. *Hhhh,*
the separated moment.

After bathing for a long time, she went through the park like a train.
"Hi," she practiced saying "hi."

[Girl compares knowing to the proprioceptive history of furnitured
wood]

I will be tranquil I will tranquilize myself in the hacienda of the topsoil. I will sift the wet topsoil in the mandibles, the mandibles proffering the man who wants to come on my face his salt liquid stinging my eyes he wants to energize with a delicate movement doing on the graft part doing the indigent thrust, I want to take down that part of hot islandic doom shifting from his assumptions where he turns his torso and then mine to make another point accessible I will hold on to the furniture the chair the gate fixated to this domicile he says provides a stability a stable I don't say I don't speak don't know what to say.

He was distant from himself except those times, he said, exponent. The language of confraternity burst from those book mouths. You tear out the pages and tuck them in your pockets, every pocket full to bursting.

Girl got tickets and rode on the bus, an amazingly bulked machine through the thoroughfares roaring and pulsing. Inside the bus was a link to personal beings rising standing crouching, the muffled electric of their clothes, the bare uniforms of their faces, a woman on the bus breathing, a baby one scrunch-faced hailing, her chest rising moist and giving wetness to the air Girl breathed inhaling.

SUB-SELECTION
She was beginning to translate – or if not starting she knew, she was turning aware, bone-graft-transitioning. *Absolutely roaring vehicles blaring.* Were the birds part of an ordinary life like skeletons of ideas tripping nearby, flocking dusty searchy with curious sockets?
The cement ripples packed in roaring, asphalt tied-down press-packed filaments grinding city city.
But from the window the sky was a flat pan understated with pink twice a day. The uncovered ground was beautiful with dirtiness, wet silty and permeate.

[SHE PRACTICES VEHICLES AND MOIST BODIES, EARTH SEMEN AND LUNGS]

Was she a cartilaginous substance all morning long, exchange rate really, putting things in and emitting them from her mouth?

The transaction zone where everything was quiet if only your ears didn't work in the regular way – you could stop and simply observe, seeing the hands deliver items to the head and the head wave and smile its satisfaction and gape in a friendly manner your direction.

All the other sounds came instead – several levels of low roar from the sky and roads around, from the pervasive waves – thuds of activity muffled in morning breaches. They all proposed to smother or define their close surroundings, their electric intentions slammed inside and water-blood shifts constantly.
And the particular sound of obligation she should listen for his footsteps on the stair.

INSIDE OUT
Gentle excitations, wavy with declension when we think of it, the broken arm on the front step, the curly hairs floating up the trees. *You know we've sat like that in time, our plans soft cloths fluttering around our arms.* When we lay between the laundry lines with sheets winding on either side, our bodies lifted like wrong ideas forgiven by the air. Doorways where we went in and out, dread on one side, holding your breath on the other. Bubbles.

He's been living this way for years and clearly expecting his identity to remain. He turns her over and over while the skin comes off and it doesn't. The entablature compiles, like you could live by adding machines = letters numbers breathing = mornings nights, "let's go to a play!" For days now they've been together "happily" and the man knows and knows, he speaks and speaks, he fairly combines nurture and project like she is one.

[GIRL TRIES TO UNDERSTAND HOW DISSIMILARITY BECOMES PATTERN]

The play is a social setting, cramming a long period in its place with descending surfaces. Bumpadump, the little gathering jostles. Her body tensed with sitting, wet on the hot plush seat.

The curtains are pushed back, the room is crowded with anticipatory bodies each one holding in its pee or trembling in unfamiliar capillaries. The blossoming out of the tendrils of pore flesh, smells Girl places now, she "understands." It was an exciting event, like a movie you "honestly didn't know the end of" or a wrestling match between two countries that had never met before. Each person sat facing forward down the benchy seats, and two men at the front hit go.

The play had expectations, they rolled their eyes extremely. Girl moved, slightly waving, the little holes for breathing tightened in.

Attached to the invisible pillars in the room were long trains of moods or cumulative events or prejudices or rejected desires or particular moments of failure or dreams of stasis or site-specific beliefs or bulky repressions surging out. Each time she repeated a word, softly inside her mouth, it fanned across the tips of those invisible trains and waved back again slowly, in irregular patterns, as though it were a perfect possibility to at least touch the broken audience assembly without any real idea of a consequence. The round square pulsed inside itself suppressed.

The dolls waiting to pee were screening, they tittered and looked forward in the line, the glass harmonics flowing over them as they touched their hair and faces with wet eyes, they emulated the posture of the situation, ah *ah I get it*. The play decides for itself. It speaks without your answer.

[THE CONSISTENT-EXPECTATIONS MAN TAKES GIRL TO A THEATRE]

BIRDS, VEHICLES

The whole frame cloistered. Not getting one on electric trees, on wires, on the tips of leaves, on her eyebrows, on fingertips, birds on plates on tables, birds in air interstices birds on the wing, *flung in the water, soaking, sobbing lightly, darkness all around their legs, eating the birds, birds whistling to tunes egress, birds sop up the bread birds on beds, birds in time and patience trying sleep* birds given to tiny manacles, on the topmost peak slight slow, the deep crest bowed for what you learn for err.

Not that there were comparatives for the situation, meshed together unseemly and speaking more all the time, the syntax more unclouding discoveries or inventions or creations of motives and opportunities we define as natural plans. Conversations were fast troughs sliced through temples, weaning for the break, electric agreement or disagreement *my hands fixed objects* on the shared parenting of the man's story, the guns speeding tight inside the hood *my mind flexed on it*. He means what he says though it collapses. Yes to eyes in repair, to brace holds and the lines, getting in the car, the engines coming on again constantly. Hhhh.

Driving with extensions of themselves inside the adored vehicles veering from one car to the next in fast dibs. These ones value this kind of thing, telling those stories like body expansion, so fast and heavy you could become then walk away. It isn't so much clarify as add and "pack it in." And the increments of action fatalistic, apparently night and day for the weaving mans.

The water fell *way, awa, thick light* away and this was air. Girl curved around her body as far as possible, the little holes for breathing licked taut barbs. Salt baths at night and the dark. Her tongue was tendrils like moist life and she licked her arm at night for contact, for continuity.

[GIRL CAN SMELL HUMAN DREAMS. HER PERCEPTIONS ARE INTERPRETIVE]

CLOTHES HORSE
Is it funny to have help where there is none, everyone's moving. She's being smiled at. Divesting as in undressing, the wind hovers whooshily though trees cannot escape it, some birds are happy to have no homes (*we have to guess, we have to imagine it I mean you can't actually talk to them they shriek at you their brain water thriving perfectly in relation*).
"You have some funny ideas" but never for too long, humans postulate in conversation – but friendly, atavistic, not there for too long the hair going brightly with the sun and eyes imperfect in self-solitude. *The flat bush gone for tendrils, flat walking pain on it, the legs talking generously to the wood, tiny whooshing flooding into the seams.*

"DON'T YOU TALK?"
Girl starts with clues: she wishes things were woolly or magnificent (*does that work*). The exchange of wet ideas reached her via persons and she reached it back.
Here, here I am, the I equating raft for salt-rise bending upward between earth and air and water, the mixture of your eyes when you ask that.
It's all happening at once. The raft between electric poison and the cooling equation of touch, the deep structure hurricane of stilled habit pulsing inward.

Sexed, it was "sex," so really it was really, the water was "really it happened" the failure of his system was an unplanned breaching of the intact wet. Strange nice man with skin like dampened bread. Pulling at the skin coming really in the wrong colors.

Okay okay silence – "I don't know you," prodding the shape of his body. Taking a walk, she sucks the sea feathers for the chemicals, for the gathered cancel of trace.

[IT HURTS TO WALK. THE CONSISTENT-EXPECTATIONS MAN ACCIDENTALLY DIES]

THE BAG WAS ATTACHED TO THE PIANO
But she took it anyway when she left, lifting it up, the white excuses
learned motions being too much to resist. *White as in the color-less
parameters of pre-linguistic fuselage, resist as in the armor of her skin trysting
bluer and more blue.* Enough to carry in one hand and no more, leave
the other free to act. Like the musical chords that touched her fingers
without hitting, like going one direction after the bus she got on went too
far and she was curved with fret, the changed diffraction of light, her
perception lessening with that, her clothes a jumble.

She had scarred his instrument with little flicks, jambles, her skin raspy
against it, holding it under her chin and plucking with her fingers, the
long strings deep and reverberant, the soft cover hitting. Where to next?

The roads were crossed, she took the piece of paper from one driver to
another, the widened road peeling the time it took. Smiling without men
attached.

[GIRL LEAVES TOWN BY BUS]

TWO
[RAMSEY]

VISIT

This new place has good light. People move in all directions in a closed area; a dog barks in the lounge, a living pillow manifesting hunger, a peppy object thrown a daunt degree.

We'll have a lunch arriviste "hi"; *hello*.

On a table some objects are poured down, the hands hover smiles. *It's me*, given to sacred attitudes, performing for a self.

"Gee whiz and here I thought." "It's past time gets us larking in the skeletons of our twin," pushing on the buttons of similitude with a remote made out of corpses.

Button, button up! "Drink up."

Where exactly is culture? The first visit of a slave to its manifold.

"Hullo love," *you are a strange bird*; you are the girl of my wet dreams, you arrive and I don't know what to say; would you like something I'm going to fuck; "I always wanted to get to know you better" *(balls of magnetized steel perpendicular to I think not and a prayer, do you know it with your breath say it with your breath, I went to sea I want to see).*

Girl is a little gangly and para-nourished, *hhhh*, not given to the dawn decree of blanch, not a custom, *the sun pushing open your eyes* with licking lips. *Hush now, the ringing in your ears is turpitude, the divine austerity of body*

[THE NEW SETTING IS DISPERSED IN HER PERCEPTIONS]

31

regimens – "ha hah" –
the symbol you carry its own incorporate pulse, pulse.

The table the chairs the sofa the implements. Eat eat. Not a problem.
She speaks of nothing in accents that trill, kissing with assembly and
outsider. *If I were to inhabit that lexicon,* she of arms. Rather to push the
diamonds, the dress shirt, padded legs, the song in the van next to the
swimming pool, the tents in the backyard, Girl looking.

Umbrage umbrella, rain in the sun, given to a soft point of view that
doesn't interrupt. The full wire mesh pushed across your back is a
semblance, a pillow. The backside attitude of life to its decrees.

One thing ends and it begins again.

At the beach
"What are you learning from social monikers?"
Girl would rather the silver box inside her head than the man at the gate,
the rocks made out of mountains in the eyes of her shiny head camera,
the lithe liquid permanences striding. The waves are indebted to the
wind and moon, the ships to the wake, that body to the towel and sand,
the head to its body, the state to red thinking. Lips are made for talking,
kissing, closing, opening, looking, smelling, eating, erupting, spitting,
whistling, licking, forming, cooling, redding, glistening, crimping,
softening, closing around the teeth, pressing, uncertain in the air when
she was sleeping.

We've gone for mid-day ice cream. *My idea is to saturate the polyphones* with
wetholds, to inhabit the eyes with questioning to peer inside the skin to
figure by disfigure mirror neurons. The *nothing* that is there is *everything,*
smiles the man without saying so. And turns the paper, The Daily Other.

[Dialog, objects, house-scapes, landscapes]

Have you seen the circumference of one living space against another, Girl was asked in words that were clearly meaning *something in addition.* She pushed her fingers into the holes in her head. *He pulls his skin one direction to deny it, the shell peeled toward a temporary octopus the hearing of experiment, he wants to help me, wants to teach me how to talk, how to ask for what I want. I want to touch inhale expel envelope pursue. I want to saturate the air world wet.*

This time Girl is shivering with the wet, her skin disfigured by multiple postures, massaging her body daily for its shapes. Go out, go through the door wet. Turn a direction.

DISFIGURE
She got a calendar magnet at the alternative print-making factory, which is really a glorified name for the work she's started in order to "earn" money, *you've got to do it,* the car drives all over the thick wet paper to make it pulpy and flat, the words distend. The rubber tires make perfect heavy flattening. All over the tires the words print themselves, the asphalt rendering them. You've got to do it. The thick paper makes for absorbing surfaces, the ink sinking in; it's a small factory with –
The visitor laughs, what is he doing.
Girl watches as unique desuetude unrolls itself all over the print in love. *Hhhh.*

The paper is bulked with its psyche, pleased with the ink seeping in, retching itself forward to the cement, talking to it, ready to push, to care. Paper cured out not regular those dimensions: what we want, what we strive for, aim for. The people working at the factory communicate their designs. Blank words cure, smooth tripping there in a gazebo pledge, all afternoon the lover flagrant for himself at the pledge, *the water necessarily underneath the buildings being held down in advance of sanctuary,* what you would give for sunset and an edge.

[GIRL IS HUNGRY, TRYING TO FIT IN. SHE TAKES A JOB MAKING PAPER]

She's still watching him. We hear about how ages depend on size, whether you should keep them or release, large for eating, medium for observation, small for all encompassing. *From a high-tech longitude platform enormous tires* bigger than the man, flattening the thickened paper platform wedge whirr whirr.

Girl lives on that walking, her peristalsis as oxygen press through the little holes for breathing, a motive as meeting reckoning that's what gets you going, the man pressing, tattoos on the skin she'll come to recognize. This one.

ARRIVAL
Lovely like that. The zone of movement is like a stage that follows and precedes you, as the world comes in to being when you move.

Day begins its long collapse, behold, the miracle of vanishing! She smiles with a stitch, the cars and soaps and limbs set, the flesh ready to open and pronounce. All the bacteria are ecstatic, making their world then exploring it, your runnels forward fondling with the dearest love of chemistry.
Sure it's a language, wait and hear! He knew the player by the tune he kept, soft magenta whirls in the air nearby the flower garden he says he always walked beside. On the way, pass her around.

The next day Girl sits on the bench in a dress made of cardboard, her figure upright flattened, lovely. The cardboard was immensely colored, as though he could not have an idea of how it was flattened without suggested marks. Blue, green, yellow, pink, red, orange, green, white, flowerets, twins, tendrils, the thyme-leaf bluet in darks of her eyes peeking massive oubliette. He had come to the place alongside her. This time Girl chose not to hide.

[GIRL FALLS IN LOVE. THE PAPER EXTENDS HER SENSATE PSYCHE]

Don't leave me

She had nothing to "get" from there, no thank you. On balance, we kept fiddling. He was a musical instrument not ready to define himself, and the latter half of life smiled streaming in his plans, as though feeding in the corners again like roulette gardens, jaded and ivoried with clasp seats you might get. Each molecule hums within an idea of closure, the soft pleasure seeking to extrapolate, dusty with tangents.

All very well for you. *We walked forward more slowly than we had ever walked,* having already sent our message. Needing permission to dwell with someone he knew. "You don't need that heartskin, Girl, whatever they tell you is décor. Here's some language to keep near your skin, to burn you when you're really feeling bad." And he kept talking and talking you can imagine; you come to expect that.

Car

Because they now had plans they kept the books in order, fretfully grown up. She had learned never to cross her legs on the seat, whose needs were for distribution over the course of a visibly defined event. *You need to keep the veins and arteries apart, to let them current.* Untwisting whenever possible, the legs are giant creatures, moving in hereditary array, the seat against or for them, the hairs on the legs tugging, individually sharp.

Floating along the very soft causeway, some of the things were "not so much," some worthy, as she called "Hello, we are getting there." Said in a soft voice nicely to her externalized cochlea, said in a never formulated voice that would not shriek or listen.

A motorcycle balancing on her thigh in the rush, "Air, air modulations! Stage coaches made of air! The gulping and provident clarity!" Laughing she laughed Girl breathed and laughed.

[Girl laughs for the first time]

Ramsey

He was really a completely unreasoning creature with hopes for a
swing, a hinge, a collapsing metaphor whose historicity would reveal
him to be not a pawn after all, not a bit stuck in the needle he was really
a threaded enormous put-together. The scissors went amazingly through
the thick material, in and of the factory. He pulled her out. He, now he,
now He was a *prince*.

His question was reverential, in hints and without attribution or without
the sounds she currently heard playing, the seaside baying near the man
with the tiny guitar whose ears were welded to her mouth this time and
hers to the scene. Fun fun, he was jangling, barring, eucalyptus with
little padding, the children waiting, the stitches on her leg so tender. She
could see endlessness rolling in as rhetorical pattern, mortal heredity as
"forever" something recognizable though not *for sure*. Every wave was
the head of her mother, the genitals of her father wetly flapping.

Revelation

A book she picked up in the doctor's office promised her she would not
be in this town forever. She read it tenderly, missing the import but
inventing a new series of events that tied quite nicely with the insistent
sounds that were flat against her waist when she tucked the book inside
her home-made dress to think of later. The nurse was a female. The
doctor was all ears, *I bet you totally wanted to bite them,* and the exchange
value of their talk was far from the book pushing into her flesh. At home
she accidentally slept with it, rolling over on the bed on the pages whose
ink made no transfer.

City walls

Try it this way, the now invisible half-wall around a town you can no
longer see though she feels the magnet thread. That robbery this way,
rivulets of wind, the lengthily visiting hoarders nodded forward, as

[Animal actions make chemicals trace everywhere. Why animism is
simultaneity]

36

though transmitting the function she herself had become in this landlubber life. *I mean the houses and flats were not so much houses and flats as the end of one stink and the start of the next.* When you get very close up to them the wet grounds among the living are chemical limits. Seas of inappropriate smile greetings, the bottom of the shoes quite visible, the naturalized cultural expectation tattooed on the inner eyelids of the denizens. They shut their eyes to "see the truth," they're constantly *transmitting*, eyes open, mouth open, body open, on the move. Rip here to match the nib with scratch, not realized in what you drink have another, how it comes through you oddly blown, slow spit through a long distending electric squeeze, paring of the eel parts in the dark. All the limbs glow at night. Her lips like eel parts in the dark.

HOMUNCULUS

She was born, apparently, into a series foretold in a loop – imagine her thick skin shedding, pulsing through – the couplings as reinsertions of skin into itself by way of another, event structures unclear in a totality but taken with a non-accumulating acceptance. *Hhhh.* Kindness begins in the inviolable skin, the chafing of the frontal part against her mingled shark-embedded animal.
In the dark pool at the borrowed swimming hole at night, she turns in the water to breathe – her cells and eggs and infestations burgeoning, repealed as youth in mottled carbon cream. She licks her skin to move the story forward, accepting the unpeeling toward him: hence Girl unfolds, recurs as presence, through her prince.

Standing by the door in shirtsleeves with the birds singing double-time for crackers we threw to them to test the weight of air against the incredible nature of our arms.
We sang too, but softly so as to not perturb the stander. Hmmm, mmmhmm, mhmmhmemm. The belt was broken on the vehicle, it shucked and shucked myriad.

[THERE'S NO SUCH THING AS RIGHT TO BE. YOU LOVE ANOTHER'S LIQUID.
EXPERIENCE MAKES ROOM FOR YOU]

Don't hold my hand don't intertwine the fingers.
He means well through the water in his eyes and hands, effusing. Diving
in the pores through stretched out sweat, tearing close. The contextual
differences of rooms and other areas was very dear. You stand someplace
and the atmosphere moves around you and makes a pocket that's your
shape, that's where you get to stand. The pieces shape around your idea
of where they fit, though air is every bit as much liquid, *so you say.*

Nice walls
"This is nice, this could be worth it." Her lips were curling upward.
So pretty there with turgid rivulets, so slaked on the seasonal combine,
so guaranteed with a solace we uptake with chemistry we all thought,
waiting for Girl to arrive with her arms full of shells again picked up
from the ground around the dusty targets pegged for shots.
When we see her we know what we mean. This is where she had been newly
born and to it she recurred, the numbers gelding whose advice developed
with the holes in her head through which she generates response.
Ahhhhm. That was the season of spring, limbs like mare. The hole in
her gender. We were to further ourselves alongside her hefted, a small
mountain between us and the sea.

Several days on, Girl stood and sat and lay down got back up and
walked and went outside and looked back into the window and walked
around several blocks near the story outline on the asphalt by the school
by the pegged mailboxes by the slight horizon of the hills that were really
mountains unlike those *mountains* really *hills* – the mailboxes were silver
squares, four by four and eight by eight, they tottered on the necks of
waiting by the playground equipment with the purple and red dissections
she talked amongst herselves and returned by way of the parched grass
to the wooden staircase fine in the aridity back up. Her skin here was
the outside boundary of impossible transfer or exchange. Nothing could
go in or come out these clothes. Teeth teeth.

[INCREASED UNDERSTANDING RESOLVES NOTHING CLOSER TO GIRL]

PERKY

Her face had fallen off and she was groping around to get it. The men
attached to her were floating in the air on giant tethers, she struck
talky since they were far enough away *hello hello*, she found her face and
hatched it back on upside down, it twisted easily and the strings get
close she wiggles she undoes the notebooks strapped to her side and
begins to strip out pieces of paper floating up for consider, renewal. The
giant earth is tentacles, is hologram.

STRING BURN

My fingers she called *my fingers whoop when I use them* they shelter the
hands near them they are captured fish they furrow and always recollect
the interstitial holding frets the friends I audit love for filler names we
bring together and sell out, in the sense of *my voice being like those I hear*
and my fingers like ten moons shining roundly at me *when I pook them up
to my eyeballs* she said.

EARTHRISE

Where is it? When she walked on the moon in the center of the painting
there it was. Her feet shushed into the smooth dust imprint, she got
down on all fours her hands, she knelt down with her torso pressed, her
frontal pressed down fully touches the tiny barbs of skin met with the
tendrils of the crescents of the items of the moon.
It had taken this long to get the point undone, the permission stitched
in the actual uniformity. It's "art." The moon in the wet sky heavy air,
"Let's take a ride."

The wind noise flat against their molded heads, torsos like the animals
bent backward when you kill them backwards *but it's all for a reason it
is reason-able.* That speed with resistance and closeness, what is that
reaching, the man with "wanting to be together," her smiles cascade

[AN ART EXHIBIT ON THE FLOOR PRIVY TO THEIR RELATIONS]

across the inside of her helmet, beaming back inside her the beam traveled to a pitch. The motorcycle burned her lower legs that hurt already from the coral teeth and punctures. The continuity of a moment was dispersed in water as it could never be in these demarcated merciless light-shift airs. The scenes smacked by light hit speed, she couldn't swivel her cartilage fast enough for sense. The motorcycle stood for the man, her angle flagrant.

BLEEDING
Love pouring from her veins the metric being achieved. The liquid forms the giant tethers, the men like balloons floating up there, the city fortunate in having no tall buildings people who are all so tread. On her feet armies, carving through the volunteer dirt.

[GIRL FALLS]

THREE
[Salt]

NEW NEIGHBORHOOD

At a space between buildings where the bee turns sideways over the
words on the ground she has between her smiling hot as lidded hides in
folds. Girl has nor waning love trick fancy on the top and striped with
loofa holdings; she tries tickling it and her deep flesh takes the sting with
curiosity. There's a water view. She'll take it! There's a skin growing
underneath the skin she can see, the thick underlay from bending.

Far more urgent than this "death" is the matter of discovery, How do bodies live
here? They protrude toward each other and their Feelings wonder something,
a Horizon clearly broken constantly in their heads, their eyes then constant
strangeness to themselves. They clearly think an X supposed to be that they will
reach and climb to formulate, dense questions over the back of one bridge and
another without fail.

Girl speaks without ambition flags over her eyes, looking at the fenced
guests, palmate hussars, dragonfly wastes – wings delaced, popped
legs, eyes collapsed – scattered near the university in town. They are
finishing the building nearby and her tassels keep getting tangled in the
architecture when she passes. The lid curls are arterial in the faces she
goes by, glancing with their own ideas passing, looking at her to cover
her with ideas. The tiny holes for breathing diagnostics.

[HER SHARK-SKIN TENDRILS OUTWARD. HALF-TOPICS OF EXTEROCEPTION]

Her hands hold out precise lines, blood lines blue, her eye grains in the
vessels, tiny valves in the lenses looking at the sun in the harnessed
trains of her face, its half-tread kind of – released, the skin trawling
derisive abnegation, seeing a woman with a phone on her ear in the
reflection across the street, teeth officed, the local gardens upright
with the lines historically ghosting, you can smell them, the poke of old
exultations mixed right up with the sparrow hawk who pesters out your
light: "straight out dive!" *Hhhh*. This town has duration, the moon over
the storefront asks for ruddy boys, scoping nervous Girl, raspberry seeds
dropping slowly out from her hair.

RAMSEY AGAIN
Café mirror unbelievably tight surcease – open the door, haste to say
the two-car-train let's catch it – bring those things shooting up from
yourself, the long legs longing on the folded man: as usual his mouth full
of haste, spiked with great custom. *Since events do not live in history* take
this crank attached to lawless improv and make yourself a better one
while you're here, the champion stalls on the way to the middle town –
"here's your ticket I bought it for you."

She and Ramsey sit on the ground her legs as soon as they enter earth
are liquidy but he can't see that and she hardly knows, supposing a
metaphor obtains in the decadent upending of the grass. They've taken
a long walk and found the organized chaos of "natural" things in a park.
Very near, a tiny animal mother is shaking for her dead offspring whose
chemicals waft upward together with the mother's; they silt the wet air
with tiny flecks of grief that enter Girl's body. She sneezes and cries; it's
about hardly knowing why that shifts in between any conversation she
might successfully have with the ordinary entelechy of a "day." She licks
her tears away from her lower face, her pink tongue on the mottle of her
skin. The strawberries and the tentacles are softer than anemones.

[HUMANS DECOUPLE FROM THEIR BODILY WILL, SPILLING ON GIRL. RAMSEY TRIES
TO MAKE HER WANT]

The whole evening Girl stays on the rocking chair. *The force holding me is like a damp steel blanket holding my ideas in place, holding the bristled skin of my mother, the patient air keeps trembling in a measure of loop. A swirl of cur hold glows dense, you chew it off and love.* The skin blanket held down the muddy hillside, small houses sliding downstream *what do you wager* everyone who passes in odd fancies watched as the road cut through the town, choked on endevilment, while inside strong forces turning up the flue and stoking the fire that made their legs too hot.

"Get the ordnance, let the fire out," emergency, emergency; the hex dome let his flat face tell you stories of the naturalized world, try to convince neutral agency, gently weep. There is neither fault nor floundering as the scene continues in the same pace she explains. It was the exact moment of the body stopping its moves, that she could tell from the wet electric, slowing. Sleep.

COMBINE
She gets a job she works flat-headed for *centuries* (days), not to entangle or yield or have average relations *I always sing now daughter, cinching with my nerves,* rocking horse, each rid and champion for stalling with the hay down near. What every woman.
Then every error she hid had flesh in it, curtains trembling, her employment skewered on the moment of the carriage ride her legs tucked in the retro blanket woo gone in the toes. Her hand held the thin edge evidently sidereal, the wooden buildings cool weave tight against the walls. No more miniature whip machines moving wet, no more clocking out, *num num,* eat it when it's given to you, the snack bars the salt-back cracker hits bite hard.

"Well they'd just throw the seed on the ground here, wouldn't have to do anything at all." *Say it again.*

[TIME PASSING AGENCY AND TRACE. GIRL LEARNS TO LAND SLEEP]

With other women in lines they walk upward, huffing like a black rectangle Girl in her cue aroma blue arms ready for tall ideas over dinner: silver unionists, campadre commentaries of performed art. A woman transacted by numbers half-conveyed a-causal "so many people to please post-Venice" *the piano caved back fallen from its platform the museum shut in my face the man holding the bundle of papers he wants me to deliver, so many people to please post-Venice* a colony of listening everywhere "home," the words collected in glass tubes and flamboyantly inquisitive markers.

Look at the man who's just rung off his best beloved turn pornography's fine wheel, the ticker tape on its paddles flaps ideas of the heavenly toward its tides, *I could do you had you stuff enough.* The little holes for breathing concentrate hard on misadventure rings, their backs "like hopping sue and lolling lily" at all times of day while choking back her earlier learned routines. Dimension's flagrant conversations extrude the length of horoscope, anatomy, taste. A shape forms past her, it moves familiar. Grey-blue it's a dress.

Girl forms her mouth on words, she takes them out and pushes them toward one attendant and another, wet and blocky. "Nice to meet you / pleased to meet you / what are you doing here / where are you from" *what do you smell like you have eaten salt in your mouth there are teeth they are leaning outward as you breathe toward me, would you like something to eat to smell to.*

Chemistry
The beakers and love's causal paddles turn gently to many pleased performances, not that Ramsey has much patience but what choice is there?, over balloon adventures and missing silos they discuss bodies in that city, much like a break from life that movie with the horse dealers bronco-busting the perihelion tidal rungs are known for. Her nose is everywhere on her mother's body, perfect corduroy smelling salts

[Words as visual images. Humans crowd Girl with difference]

beneath our seats, replacement lily walks her best idea toward the rushing sound of dinner half-remembered in this run, the sweat adventure pulls them out. The *salt of the earth* is the semen of the father: it says right here, the ground is full of it.
"Are you individual or species?"
Which aspect of your flesh do you encounter either way you ask the question. If you read this book or if you read that one, even balanced they admit they haven't learned to set their teeth on critical distance.
"They tell you things and then there's what you actually do."

The various streams within the airy water had nothing we'd call names though they could have done, like Beginning, Inkwell, Bloodstream, Mother: names, titles, labels, handles on the sides of every body.

WHITE ROCKS
The continuous lake waves built on brave involuntary choices running through her legs and *splash*, she ends up walking at the white line chuffing avidly (recalling something) conveyed by listening bleachers whose asylum lolls on seasonal ticker tape of distant edges, the archery of round routines flicking up her legs beside the boards that Ramsey's most enamored of (a wholly private thing, she reasoned, breathing narrow floating buildings without visible turrets on the ground) to make him adjectival, geared with heighted love.

The silent chain formed itself around her torso, up her throat, pulling at her tongue, it meant she could never really speak with the full injury of all she might, the lolling qualities keep it parsed, partial, her thick neck gropes. That untranslatability being the half-slipped land-slide kind of "person-hood" she's noticing in the other body eyes and talk she hears conveyed. How do they keep from fundamental loneliness?

[GIRL TRIES TO BRING WORDS CLOSER TO ALL THE THINGS THEY'RE NOT. HER CARTILAGE TIGHTENS]

Having decided, Girl moved there. She was clawed in time with barque masks. She collects herself for a while, herself several damp examples leaning on the pulpit by the end of the rented hall, and she would give them up next time she felt herself leaving town. But the hall was comforting, it was renewable and unlikely, her slapping feet from one end to the next.

The hot wine drunk down her throat. To be alone and yet populated with exemplars was an aim she was learning to adopt alongside books with lists of names, one anchored to the next and the next, one heaving according to time, another according to license or locale, another simple alphabetical comforting. She had these by her strange eating, piece by piece, piled thin. The sniffing of the skins of the books taught her how to think and speak here.

MICROCHASM

The throbbing in her innards, clay-like push on the toilet: was this death, making an early apparition? No no, water everywhere wearing its drink breath, sods of healing while dissimulate, salt, fluids, tiny creatures, scales at the eyes, the limbs, the mouth. The barrier no soft nor hard thing, only something against the red pressure of the retained self-mode, this moving thing she was within throb throb, the blood inside like airplanes pushing slowly across a thick sky.

So, the pull from one side to another achieved as a question of lunar cycles!, *the periodical*, or blood chuffs, ears yearning one direction then another with the pull of a story whose hook gave it a mouth that latched to legs and pulled, the ink follows the story cycles, the blame and watching, will she swell; will she absorb all that and swell? These were logics or fashions she learned, looking out over the media cycles, astounded. The peeling back of eyelids to learn the wet infestation of images. The peeling back of the vagina to see the coral ambient there,

[GIRL MENSTRUATES FOR THE FIRST TIME ON LAND]

astonished thick colors, curling her whole body around in a circle toward the vagina, pushing the fingers, pushing in the extruded anagrams of the heart, the folds there pounding.

Bleeding she opened many books and sat down in the middle of the pages leaving bloodlines. *There* was writing with the body complex! The blood gathered between her legs that were split, it was delicious. "My books, my books, you've bled my books!"

LAND STORIES

The connection between living and doing gathers ciphers, answers whose questions are not ready. Slipping's constant and these split skies horizontal, vertical. What he meant was parallel to her developed meaning coffers, the *value* they forbid. But if she went along, if she *made herself available,* things happened. At the movies she got in line, he paid for the ticket then the food; but the ticket person said *I did not pay* . . . she had no other money and opened her hands said look and see, her dress moving as she moved, wet and slapping . . . they rolled the videotape to some authoritative person and when it came to the place where she had paid the screen was blank green, slate blue. She turned to look to the distance and she held still, blank slate blue, hovering among the rough wet hills near *where the film was going to play* . . . but all the accoutrements of such things were gone.

The others were nowhere in sight, their drugs and plans storied, she and her sea friend fell to the ground gaping among the rough hills the bodies of some of them . . . the females naked and smeared across the ground, a severed appendage, a female who had slid against her earlier, wet tendrils gaping, her body smeared across the ground.

That's the movie shone on the outside wall of the theatre she sees. Intermission.

[GIRL USES HER BLEEDING VAGINA TO READ. SHE BECOMES A FILM SHE SEES]

Is this "news" or "information"? What is this? Is it coming toward or setting to the side? What is the function of this sitting act watching? No I'm serious don't correct me.

"The function is a fiction of progressive life in which you understand within a knotted frame the parallels between your own confusion and the narrative exigencies played out. That's why we watch the films, that's why we sit in repetitions of those hourly minutes."

She walked with the serious men now going somewhere. She was fully clothed in draperies and had a book that stood for her resistance and they allowed her to carry it. The more people are gathered together the crueler . . .

They came to a high cliff terrain with a dark metal ladder twisted going up and all began to climb. The cliff went on. They tried to trick her into setting down the book so they could kick it down but she was wary and caught it balanced on the rung. She was forbidden to tuck it in her skin, the book was sticky with thick . . .

the cliff ladder went on and up darkness and resting and . . . they climbed and climbed, the time perfused with dread, and never finished reaching whatever was at the top. All along one side of the bottom of the cliff was a dark defined body, one eye unsettled upward, the mother's eye. This was the film Girl saw as her mind on the inside wall.

ALLEY

After the movie in which she was without satisfactory answers, Girl dreamt the dead bodies swirling in the water. The ship was going down and the calls were gulped, the piercing of the earth via the salty wet of the dark sea. The faltering lights shone orange and creased, the walls flat with the color we think of when we think of outside walls. *Nothing happens without you, dark light within the sky.* From then on every intense suggestion swirled back in the coitus inside her brain. You're a manifest

[A LAND DREAM REPLACES THE EVENT OF CINEMA]

of charged particles imbued with forebears, demonic release, even as the sense of solitary walking covers you absolutely, with invisible potential for change, the air quiet but with a very low suppressed shrill ringing noise and with humming in the buildings' contained electric. Her purple dress flaps around her ankles in the dark, turning into tassels at the bottom where her skin tears the fabric, "natural action" as the *lacerate against culture!*

Girl walks with absolute quiet, listening for deviation from the hum and ring, her breath, her bones wet sheaving. Her standing still and looking with face to, waiting.
The side of the building beginning to glow individually, her walking next to it very slowly, the side of the building quiet, the sky seeming to be pressured back away from the light at the top.

RAMSEY
They were decanted into an alternate apartment block. Her blood flowed like wine just beneath the surface of her skin when Girl sat and watched for it. *I could see it move if I listen very closely I could hear the swish and tell.* She was picking up a little bit of different training with softer seats; she was becoming less aware on a minute basis of her skin cells rubbing off continuously, brushing on the seats, on her clothes, on the sheets turning. Living and doing things, the little holes for breathing polished smooth.

Ask me about that narrative again and the rendition is never the same. The ship was dark and sunken, the dream sunken, the calling out with impassioned invocation triumphant, my body enamored of a sieve and split by fever pitch, the clothes ditched and falling off in the turning in the water, the seminal moment hard by laws amidst the thrashed water, arms up and following along an explanation in words thereafter. As though that wave could carry forward all the way into your mouth.

[GIRL HAS A MEMORY OF HER CONCEPTION. TURNING HER PRE-EXISTENCE INTO NARRATIVE]

FOUR
[TRASH]

INFLUENCE
"The racket, man, America's tongue stuck to your mouth!"
Having only each other coming home and throwing off your coat of
mail, stoking the millennial fire with your little drum hum valley path he
sang *moana Havana heaven* cabana – in the cool nights an evocation of the
moss-grown throttle perched on the equally quantified balustrade.
"It's a great apartment." Such party language ruptures the glistening
talents Girl's identified and throws her odd ideas on the floor by drink;
she giggles, she absorbs, she has her tassels straightened for the rest of
the week she is mollified.

Fold the sheets this way and take me in, he queried, warm clay gentle
formed on her chest to convince her, linen paper in spite of lost originals
she had really written, she'd been *write*. How do you pitch over to
another side of "living," as though new. That message was already on its
way with its silly code enciphered – it is crazy recognizing *for the sake of
your own genuine understanding of flaws* as though the mountain Latin would
be missed, the way he looked not so much blue jeans as chilly isosceles.

"What are you doing?" *I have had to dis-emulate to get my honor back, what
kind of inhabitation is that saying, what corpse of human culture built those words.*

[GIRL RESOLVES SOUNDS AS MUSIC. SHE WRITES FOR THE FIRST TIME]

What those human females are talking about now otherwise, today especially in the spare curiosity of waiting it's absurd, there's a thickness to the declaration. "After writing what will you do," take the paper to the funeral of romance and show them, like truth's the irrelevant floater in your eye when the ashes are floating away?
That's the way he saw it, no doubt. You dropped the comb you lost the dark flowers. Getting back's the same as "forward." What is the accumulation of identity you're encrusted.

Words that turned toward her torso, these lonely conversations with a "good idea" or "mistake." Wet, wet and thick, dark alternative breaching in the insides of her head.

TEMP
"These are 3D objects held together with a spring-load device," said the nice motion.
Upon her inner shoulder her head sank with real tears, thin ones and sweet thought, as though from a different origin and thus displaced and not unsettling.
"When you settle them in the box be sure to use your strong hand to gauge them and your other hand to flip the last corner of the cardboard."

On the inside of her skull ideas tapped unquietly, *the girls were wont to talk about fidelity to the company which I explained saw them in no such lights.* Burned through with lessoning, the girls showed her their claws turned into painted diaries, white curves of moon, red pools of bandage. "Beautifully done" while Girl stared dislocate, her panties wet with tears. They were stupefied, inside the template of their chests their hearts beat disquiet back into the break room where they nodded with their backs to the camera.

[WRITING MAKES NEW SELF — IT PERCEIVES OR SENSES INTEGRATE]

Totem

She pointed her index finger at the wall, displaying for all to see her knowledge of the intimate link between first principles. Or so the listeners supposed. Not that anyone was there, not that it had done her any good, these distances from the shore she interrogated on paper, pretending to know, pretense as rented *head space*. Ramsey had been under the tree at the wrong time. Girl stood making marks, she sat lodging; the blocks out of her mouth were wet, handing them to an interlocutor.

Girl came to understand the latch in her locale, her distal procreation, the bark of trees or water transfer, the hiding of self in the woods, the matches wet from hurricane. She hid in the trees, understanding there had been something (the distinction between the generalized mass and the protruding other), a switch from what was potentially in awe to what was actually *so yesterday*, the malfeasance imagined as music to the ears of the disempowered, the inadvisability of driving or being seen, the embracing of what seemed like yielding in order to avoid when anybody meant that they or she or combinations could be driven to *understand*.

The reading rooms were full of a situation described as waiting when she might instead propel, that situation hovered categorically as an attitude or dissembling. An emergency point never activated, a chassis system inserted into the propellers of her temporary arms, an enginery defined as biological wizard by the off-grid, a calm identifiable as checking out. The people in the library bred their words. Yet they were kind to her in a mildly egregious disconnect, in this comfortable place where sufficient absence could produce a situation of expansion felt within and transferred to the naturalized objects labeled with a softened set of tonguey eyes. She with her special set of body always smelled like salt licks with metal bands attached for carrying, theoretically she could go anywhere carrying herself. Like she said within *move on* and then her legs went up. *Purchases, like a kiss.*

[Girl hides in the library. She listens to order]

TRASH

Lacking a shredder, she burned the papers instead. She was dressed for it that day with the windows rolled up and his name on the back of a photograph. He gave it to her sitting right there.

After a while they stood at the corners of their respective buildings, just the sight as though going to the bathroom. It was health and it was unimaginable with the instruments and the female. Her eyes were wrinkly by comparison, smiling sleek lids with the messages tattooed on the inside beaming out to Girl. She learned the maneuvers he had grown accustomed to and before long they shifted the furniture. The moving sidewalk of the will.

GETTING TO KNOW YOU

"Right here!" She pulled over at the rest area or was pulled, the driver smiling, lovely massive thing not so much a lay-by as a stopover, not so much a pass-over as a ramp for failing brakes, rather a series of sheds embellished by hope than a lean-to. The vehicle faltered slightly at the tenor of the path off-road, whose plans had maybe clearly been foreshortened by the climate of the recent past, wherein those without had been justified, the laws for failing need or weakness making just enough room for your margin slough.

The vehicle's wheels needed adjusting, she herself, the little holes for breathing tight and loosening, *hhhh*, the bugs frequenting the joint needed only promissory notes to wait with wings and legs quite patient for the failure of system. Caw caw. Birds shriek across air molecules, alongside the legs or vehicle, their communiqués directed at whom? Her spiracules protruding half-way gentle, hhhh, out from the submergence flooring of her skin. Contact and its manifest gradations: the face became a set bandage of arenas, pushed and pulled into positions needfully, smiling and talking blueful now. *And yet it is a beautiful day,* no gainsaying it.

[SHE GETS ANOTHER SHIFT JOB AND LINKS WITH ANOTHER MAN]

How can I say what it's like? Suffusions and atmospheres as my mouth makes meaning of bodies. The thick dark motion eventful without terror, given constantly, the thick dark motion rings and streams. We want to reach each thing and take it in or spit it out with teeth and tongue gulp fast. The dense electric cold.
Protruding like a disk blade, sharp on the plate of the map, edged on the eye her chances of getting anywhere *in time.*

The rental car was being driven by someone she had met three days ago, the squiggles clean and colored green and red. The squiggles on the map side, the turn toward the roadside where they stop. The road side with its *architecture* non-existent: Girl wondered about architecture, with its naturalized subsidiaries the sides of buildings planned with transaction in mind. The bodies of those who'd made each building lingering in the smell. The thing called motel, the windows shaking and shaking with the howl. Take out your harmonica and vibrate, sing.

SWEET MARIE
The next day on the bicycle, the bag on her back bore the brunt, the bag across the hills and asphalt pressed against the same spot on her back and made it gradually rise up the gentleness of the body under bending the rise of the razorback the dirt falling crumbling off the humpy rock until the wind and sun are constantly on that top like a barometer, like a rooster skeleton, like rusted leftovers of an outbuilding, like the ship high up on the desert floor with occasional visitors. Girl stays there for a long time, her skin infolded coloring. She is focusing.

She ate all the chocolates from the machine and still wanted more. She sat by the train and waited without patience. She held a book in each hand and tossed her head from one to the other, alternating lines aloud. No one joined her in the station. *Hhhh, hhhhh.* The books went on and on while crows flew near with bronze beaks from the tracks, the parting of the air without wounding or tear. The name of the next place was

[GIRL ACQUAINTS HERSELF WITH A DRIVER; SHE TALKS ABOUT UNDERWATER]

syllables, anchor, motif, here comes a train. She smiled to each book and
shut them one by one.

She's in the texts she slowly devoured in the reading room where she
kept on all her clothes. The history of nomenclature and structures
with time frames believe in themselves. This one was 1969, that was
1984, this woman was 1620, it was amazing you could be these things
absorbing them!, that one was 1905 or 1438, events were self-instructive
in 1855, she maybe 2001 hit that 926 comparatively 2004 and then
in 1632 the elements of 1446 sorted into the possessions of 1989, she
was – each thing you learn absorbing in your blood. Munch munch
Mesopotamia. *Given the constellated nature of the temporary formation of an
identity in a situation, there is no way to know anyone or anything* she learned.
But you can hover there, suturing things and traits together, positing.
Enormous voices in the stratified earth.

The pain in stating flatly your vocation is matched only by the stain
inside your brain from half-bent anchors. People hold themselves down
on tethers from the bottom of the world. They climb on ladders to make
merchandise called ceremony or the other way around. Dowsers, school
plinths, the piquancy of *facts*.
Her legs press together to absorb the urine back in.

ANIMADVERSION
On the train, she was late again paying her ticket. Stumbled to a
miraculously disappearing line, too many clothes on for some perturbed
futurity. "Sorry, sorry."

She took her bag up the narrow metal steps to the top level of the train
and in the very first compartment he was flat out on his back asleep
exhausted under covers but smiled weakly and beckoned her in. She
was there.

[HISTORY IS A TRAIN STATION]

On his machine a set of images and ear bud noises: on the camel, the person on the image swung heavily forward and then back, blond corduroy jeans aridity erases all the smells said the ear buds. *Hbhh* hm hmm ha. Filling the wet wind from the tinny vents sheening across her flesh.

I give (new job)
She explained to her new friend how much. Fortuitous hedge
I give the hands the feet leave away
I give the time again and here we are
I give the boy the door and his tilt grams I give the particular amount I give
the way we say it she said
I give the peat down moss slopes, I give the wary hammers of munificence, I give the strained waves turned toward you tumbling there, I give a wave spread a wily chamber, given she is sodden she reverts to the ultra wane, the time we slaved and did not apprehend, like a deal we didn't know we had struck.

You could stop anywhere and give your time work in the kingdom of green fear. The papers on the glass walls match the thick bodies moving that economy: this box has a set of wires, this box with lights on and singing, this one with a tower ready to go and this one "ugly as sin," this one she walks into, *and this one* –
she is ready to lean on the wall to listen to the crows, she takes the book and leans with it unprepared for the friendliness of her co-workers, they split her mind, her skin, the hatches opening on the mouths, stories that fly gleaming from the mouths, ceaseless subdivisions of encounter.

All day long the throat is stroked with feeling, the walls pale and admonitory, the wales on the wallpaper *think no thick and* hedgy. She feels them for the particular stripe, the glory worry trembled on a little, with the fingertips there by the seating areas, plates and cups and peeling

[A man on the train shows her a video. Girl stretches thin]

faces. She is not worried; she is waiting for a trial, an evidence panel, for the petri dishes to *front up*.

People are all over. The seats are arranged for optimal focus, for a lean-in, for dread solitude to yield its doors that having nothing whatsoever that *here* –
"There there you've not meant for it to happen"; he was *in the wrong place;* someone is holding her hand on one side (leaning toward the end of the bench) eschatological with flat-cakes shivery and each one like a node abrogating the current, one direction and then out, so that it isn't a joining together at all but rather an individual hook-up, like the sets of wires she reckoned from a start, the jolt gone comfortable before it's even. *Swim, swim hard after it.*

DERBY (YOU MEAN TO WANT)
A race, a set of leg wheels, a forced-air current sung afterward, Girl is tucked under the plastic wave of watching. She has a pale drink in one hand, held against her cheek, the moisture sucking fast.
Her eyes are exuding like roller-coaster warnings, she is uptown and sure of the peace of that place, having "donated" to cassowary cages the umpteen calibrations of a feather cape given to her by someone in between her legs, the seats downwind, the orchestra dulled by the wind and horses.

Nor had one made no promises in that instance.
No no. Don't worry.
The woman talking said the town was hers and always would be for it could be naught else, her eyes left rolling there in the plastic pavement saw the story before and after the wage she would be made to pay for it. People had made commitments to the event, they had given their all and left with it intact.

[THE TRAIN MAN HELPS GIRL. DEATH IS NOT HER FAULT]

The horses strained familiar, their streaking pounding sweat and nervous give. What did it mean to give, to yield? To pluck a piece fast or eventually for whom? The fountains dangle with dogs and fish and human females as she moves closer to the horses when it was over. At that moment she had nowhere to take anything down. She smiles with cracked face toward the partly friendly women.

GARDEN PARTY

Girl stood, her barometers impeccable for now, the wind shifts over the map, the sky adhering to the outlines of the solid objects next to it, the solid objects perpendicular. She could read the desires of other strangely, she pushes her skin against one of them and each part pushes back in a measure, the particulates exchanging deep and tiny. She saw and felt it, which she was learning to associate with apprehension. Each thing or happening was up against several more. It was possible to leave new sets as a counterpart to the solid objects all around her, now tenderly. The sandwich was tasty in her mouth, the gritty parts yielding sufficiency, the crunchy parts meeting the surfaces of her teeth and her tongue folding intelligently around the motions of chewing. The sandwich was churned dairy, chlorophyll, grains. The tincture of that person's blood pulses nearby.

HOSPITAL

He was dying there, someone who had given her *time*. You enter a new placehold and even in doing something wrong there was a placehold for you, someone would *bail you out* if they understood where you fit inside their story. She held his hand with a solemnity, counting on the flowers to hold up individual peaks at night, to wager him also. Constant noises announcing unexpected developments that were not houses, windows, inventions, set ideas, expectations of propinquity. Screeches and up and down elevators made your head pressure, swell, then recede again.

[AFTER THE INQUEST EVERYONE'S KIND. BAIL. A HORSE RACE]

Girl turned her head in the smells, she shook in tinily formaldehyde, odium, bright alcohol streaks. *Hhhh*. Nothing wary had happened up to now. What it meant to "mean well," someone who was pushing outward not breathing in. *What did you pick?* He kept asking. "How did you choose?" The horse had placed. Smiles like the manatee.

PUBLIC GATHERING
The bus ticket was open so she got on.
Necessarily things were left behind. It was possible to strike conversations with seated bodies and to make arrangements with them to see houses and other buildings, even ranges outside houses, shaped lands that were familiar to them. Fascinating, even actful.
When you performed they responded, as though your existence were an agent.
Necessarily things were left behind, the man in the hospital who had paid to get her out.

There were points over that hill, with the salty blood and nose caves she enounced them. Operating on the low-bar credit system, like that time she had smiled near the grand marquee in the central car, she moved slowly this time.

CLUB
Girl had traveled in a small group to get here. The struck-up traveling conversations had led to *come along,* and hey it was like a broad invite. Around here culture is like a slow-moving flash mob. The level of inviting talk was medium, sort of situational like sandwiches between meals. A gorgeous electronic truck parks at the river, a vibrating leader sporting defense lapels, the fresh water traducing sound elements he trickily desires. *Here he comes with an argument, a lonesome croon out there.* Dance, a one-story frame.

[GIRL MAKES FRIENDS BY SHEATHING HER CHEMICAL EMPATHY]

Faltering person trembling as she is removed from content, she's listening, origin settled upon *up all night before* to direct routes through the ambrosia, the land clothed with leaves proprietary water taken out of context, it was exhausting.

We have these stories, port them, an arch whose cold stone starts to talk in 3D revelations, taking the names to pasture's logical ends *here comes an argument* intervening in an old-fashioned morning, center stage a purple city cloth draped sideways by moaning parchment fairly visible, ventilated by a tithe paid to data's ardor, the fragile micro-legislants on either side of the speaker.

"Select among imperatives to be followed for a period of time. Large public meetings." *God* this was like those pieces of paper she gathered up for learning how to read, or books. "It won't be easy, commotion will easily forget, we'll leap over each other even": communed by windy cloaks, the settled persons walked in decision, holdovers moving softly in the wind.

This was a new currency for Girl, the way they moved their mouths and the air went in and out in, chest compressions that produced sound waves against each other's heads. *Your words were found and I did eat them.* The group kisses each other meaning, on the cheeks: they make room for each other in a large idea they agree on, they make music about it. They went back into town and rented a long building with rooms that went from one to the next to the next, and Girl chose a room painted red, number three.

CONTINUING EDUCATION
You're here for a while, baby, give in to it...
the time when men with kites are testing their ability to endure past the dress code... honey on her lips...

[SHE ATTENDS BELIEVERS WHO INVITE HER TO A GATHERING]

in other words, like the guarantor of technique who doesn't need to be told again his enumeration of the bear is tandem to support machines we vie for, hand over hand, mouth over mouth next to the rising values of the crops ...

... you can't expect them to know where they're going to grow, bone bridges finely fertilizing the next crew, patches sutured by literal seeing beneath their feet the hole, the seed... crop class. There's room for you to sleep here, feed.

Exogamy as wrapped in red again as though the day has already come when she'll find the term she's looking for she's expecting.

Her new friends won't need to open their eyes to read the road signs of the captive since the enormous shell she rides in overhead allows them criss-cross views at night, *splendid caves we peer in* as we override again and *I can see why she never wants to get there* at (withdrawal).

Plots and monuments folded in paper. A token abecedarian moves his bread to the other side of his China plate with fetishized adornment, the realm of the bear. He smiles without meaning too.

RECUR
Girl nodded like she'd understood. Can you stay that long? She nodded. Ramsey was back again like blood in animals. Was he the same man or a filter? The type she hardly recognized the human moving through the gradient air although she knew *they were all different* you were supposed to know that. He was trying to convince her she didn't have to complete the picture. He was training *perros lazarillos* for the local sanctuary and he came to the club because their dedication to assembly meant your body got much larger when you were all together. It was an easy thing that delineated the time and forced him to remain. Handy, like a rope.

[THIS REPRESENTS TIME. SLIPPAGE BETWEEN ANIMALS AND BELIEF]

They saw a movie about a man who put upon his life a theatre and ate pathos for midnight wastes. He could never listen to any woman who talked. His ears had tangent wax in them undiscovered until the footage was burned and the film bled wax onto the crematorium floor. They talk about this movie, Girl and Ramsey, late into the afternoon. She had hostel work, which was easy because you could smile at warm margin persons and get lots of time to read and she was starting, just starting, to draw. The staff at the café got to smiling at them. Time to go.

[Ramsey finds Girl again]

FIVE
[ROCKING HORSE]

That was a day for the pen, she rigged it, solemn after eating fish in the
tent park, hhhh. Several of them pegged for kindness upon sailing the
lake next door. The fishes lost their wishes.
Something he would never do, she wagered, with the dryness all around
in spirit, the structures of belief set up as that.

Girl was picking up talents rather than skills, needing not so much to
plug in as to *turn on* the guitar, being one item she kept from him whose
padded case provided softness for her head, clear enough so long as
there is water some place near for the hands, the arms. To feel down
to the bottom of the water, like the temptation everyone had, or the
imperative, to drill, to silt into the roots.

She swallows. It was like bone sighs, those little tender pieces of body
moving softly down her throat. It was like eating herself, she reckoned,
like being monogamous with your present body.

Look over here – she moves over to pause in front of a screen with others.
The calls come, they shoot sonic tendrils. *If I ask a question in the middle of
a discourse, why am I asking it? Provocateur.* One seepage sat next to another,

[GIRL FLEES THE MISUNDERSTANDING – SOMEONE ELSE SLIPPED TIME. CAMPING]

the microscopic tendrils in discrete sharings. This person was a newcomer organizing aspects of objects and information in friendly ways. Teacher teacher. He moved his hand across the touch pad lightly titching now and again.

We might as well admit extremist rulers as the gauge of how *long is the rope dangling from the graft. This flower is very roman, very algebraic when you press on it, and if we were to sell some produce in batches we would bolster our comfort here.* Grammar is an experience we've all had, "but how will you use yours" she hears a woman say about the vegetables.

SUNDAY
The decision comes down like a wolf on the gold of her lips (I have eaten and yet I thirst), she thought quickly: *I have hammered into the signal* the forecasts of the bed on which we sat and planned our breakfast. "What am I doing here?"
Thence oratory leading to demise. Her microscopic flesh folded gently but firmly into thinking *if thinking is accomplished by turbines nearby, by the welts of factories on my inner ears.*
Could we be made to think on the scale of burrowing wires very near the eyes that hover compromise. The torso is shaft, the thighs are salt, the eyes are olives around which your tongue rolls, the skin is tearable, the genitals are islands, the cartilage bendable, the hairs sifting out of the skin are tiny wires for pulling with your teeth.

We're all watching you, he said, a picture created by facsimile, a gorgeous temper burning small and bright *so like an angel* animate foreclosed. You don't say much with your mouth. *I will start to make a future stripped of confraternity figured in the tightly laced mind of someone else whose self-addicted laws crash in and back, a sound I recognize with a memory that might be imposed?*

[GIRL TOUCHES MEMORY – WHAT HAPPENS CASCADES]

She speaks when there is something to say. The fantasy of having arrived for somebody's approximation with a bigger fantasy nearby of songs and linkages, tried for going back, stone monuments carved out to keep the neural stock well-watered, shoots in the field with the enormous boulders where she heats the stones and knows who is not coming back. He won't come back.

BAILIWICK
Decked and clocked, cleaned and stroked, the time card settled in its pocket so she can go on break and lie like a bag in the sun, skin stripped of salty varnish, ready to roll. Her compatriots glued to the television for the latest, leaders whose tongues hang out like dogs on fire, their tails being slowly consumed from behind, the flames rolling forward like small bits of news, waste pieces, the total hunger of the ears that burn the sun whose passage much like replacement parts can make a mock-up elocution the whole square would listen to, but for the hostel kids whose tempered smiles like cubicles can soothe her parching skin. Go back. Skip bail. Don't go back. *Go back.*

She has no money, she must forage in her baggage, the wet insides, the leaves. The little holes for breathing speak their parts inside her ears wet tiny. Click click, click click click. The red door, beyond which is the sea. Her new friend suffused her little holes for breathing. On the forest floor she pants, she coats herself. Her new friend is on the speaker, is the speaker, Token. *Hello.* Hello hello. Girl smiles.

She slowly attaches objects to the inside of the tree, largesse. A pan, a little glass, threads. Token has a truffle pig, what?, a mushroom trowel. Her skin ripples inside at night, inverted tendrils prickling out blue blood maps she chews by day. Each morning she leans forward, sits up. There is a little water nearby, and she has legs whose damp surety consoles her.

[THE PRESENT INTERFOLDS WITH PRIOR EVENTS. IN THE CAMPGROUND GIRL GETS HUNGRY]

67

She finds a book on a wayside and is happy because it has nothing to do with anything she knows. Her new friend laughs at this one, stretches down the smallest trees to lie on. *What what, when one does not entail another necessarily, I mean you choose to swim together?, is it like that* he pulls at her, he does not strangle harvest.

TRIP MACHINE

Gaunt with elbows skinned from dreaming of past food, she moved slowly through the market desiring. (The market did not exist but was a desire module in her mind, the stalls and umbrellas shining softly.) She would imagine things other than the maggots in the potatoes, the *Santa Claus* at the back door of the apartment. Too rangy, not equilibrated at all. Someone had taken the battery out of the car and left the hood up as a sign, as though you would walk away in the middle of a conversation but gently touch the body of someone who could no longer be there. Not broken the wires though, the visitor had just needed something. Token liked talking story; he was a new person who helped her in her quest.

"Could an end point be called a quest?" After all no one "believed" her and it was not a question to be entertained, that gutter in the field where the cows walk or the sluice in the dark gyre stream the breached wall. The correlate between the words and her reaching out toward you. That was in the fabric of the heavy air, that correlate.

The tree was gangly over her head, it cocooned her and the small mammals that passed by hungry, the birds and righteous insects.

"What do you mean, we?"

LULLABY

Hhhh, mmmmhhemm, mmmhmhmemmm.

I lay my head on sleeves warm leaves, the book spoke itself out to her, sitting there leaning against the tree. The fuzzy air left uptake on her inner eye, the read and starry syllables were all furry on her tongue.

[UNDER THE TREE, GIRL AND TOKEN TALK STORY]

She hasn't spoken much today, tired within and food without the wind a lasso crimped her hair, the febrile ground a trip machine, a door without an in between. The tree is not vigilant.

The literate machinery spoke its name to Token who was a willing and gentle magnet principle gathering filaments nearby. Girl was a non-magnetized substrate, a docile presence with fervent absence squandering. The vegetables became that after they were plants, their sweet roots chewable.

When you put the coins in the machine really great ideas drop down unrelated to any present need except in your ability to apply them. Like brain plaster malleable to the cause. She kissed him, succor as an envelope's arrival. She would promise anything to a futurity whose presence was not a gift.
Yes, it is definitely harder to move on land – *but I don't understand the press, the air as implement.* And he too is all *explain it, baby, explain it and I'll show you* in a stroll taller than the wooden bridge that charges you to walk it. Bend down through, *baby*, bend down.

ROCKING HORSE
Out back, someone said we define a day by one occasion in it … making a meal, celebrating an event or anniversary, having a conversation you remember, achieving a limited objective …
putting stuff out, tearing at the horse, the stuff on his back neck where the mane would be, it's fabric made thin on the wood, he's beautiful …
he was someone's, someone she knows now, the music drafting across the river town with its shops, the horse swaying back and forth in limited arcs, the rocking soft, the threads tearing out from the back of the neck, feeling nothing he is riven, it's a he she's sure …
I remember a meal, the river is making a medium rippling sound very near her on the porch of the building, the horse smiling in wood, Girl smiling grim, done, detasseled.

[DISLOCATION BETWEEN HER OWN AND COMPOSITE HUMAN CHARACTER]

They walk together, the evening is coming on. The tent is defenestrated and she's tired, this time he curls around her backside without asking, pushing aside her coverings, fur, penetration, the licking pant of the dog, pushing as she moves, squeezing asking sweating; then she's sticky in the vaginal canal.

LAND BITTEN
What was that thing that settled down and needled on the off-chance she would not detect and empty it that settled down on the off-chance she was not in her right mind and warrior on the chance that she had not selected society here on this spot what was the needle that befriended her tiny portion of flesh that was organically inspired that had left behind the ichthyus sensations she was after what was that – was it foreshore clemency coming for the red salt was it ironic detachment feigning need was it rigorous genetics applying itself was it engineering canceling all but one direction was it unity via a portal. She didn't know and couldn't, she was getting to be sure. It was thick like what he tasted of when she turned back her mouth.

She took a drink by the shore and spat it out and spit again to wash the taste from her mouth. No salt at all, just silt that came from registering paddle boats, manure, the oil from bird feathers, the gestation of tiny frogs and fishes, the slow decomposition of sticks at the bottom the remainder of bottles cans rocks dirt slides trade boats fallen hair fallen leaves roots. Girl would have to hunker here, have to train. Her medial vocabulary sifting slowly down through her torso, cells growing wetly homing large.

On the move again, she's been walking for miles in the water and her legs are interface, a percept, *hhhh*, miles across the microscopic terraces lifting up her feet, every field underscores the part of the ground that fringes the city suffering under media umbrellas.

[GIRL NAMES LAND QUALITIES, WORKING ON HER INSIDE RELATIONS]

Girl is close to a time when being there's to reach whilst earthy creatures blink at the top of the air at what's been – like scalped, *some thing you like or don't* the beat beat tucked, a woman with a parasite inside her rolls by where that little flesh is growing stretching its arms and legs over the dainty bones of its hostess, darling, the world is made for flesh your rawness here is tender, blank spit undone while furled and akin we find attach. *Drink this, there's been a storm, the sandbags are here to help.*

And she turned a corner inside her body for she had new seed, that man having joined her blood (he was a squanderer), they had slept on the ground together she going puffy the blankets the thinnest stuff the tent so small they tucked their heads under going down. She knew before how to retain it but now her body's grown in architectures of air and the porous skin between. *In the water, all that time, she and the little one romped in imagination's term.* She would slip out and the salt would sting her eyes gelatinous with a change of scene, the outward and visible sign would be eaten by the mother in search of nutrients, the electric pulses clamp the water excitedly. Sway nearly near the mother, soft raspy grasses down below the ground, the mother's liquids choose.

But ah not that way, no way, no thank you way not yet. Girl smiled in her shell gland covertly, you could come onto the earth and you could learn as something. Simply wait, store the stuff until then, pushing around her insides tendril pockets, so then *so then the seed thank you yes I'll trow it, truck it till we're ready, till we have a home imagined in between.* Far away for a reason, the penis was like an infant with one eye to eat.

VAGILE ANIMAL
She was movacious movalicious she was tantrumy and she studied the implication of Sanskrit and she waved her arms and she was ready to redefine belief as the substance of intense encounter and release and

[SIMULTANEOUSLY, GIRL IS A BLUE SHARK. HER SHELL GLAND STORES TOKEN'S SEED WITH OTHERS]

the little holes for breathing were in constant contact with the elements she was always touching without textual promise on balance on a non-steady nor lasting series of touch points who were true to her because that was contact.

The dog explained things after she pinched his tail and he bit her she didn't understand the connection between her actions and the recipient nodes of an other she was aware only of the missing element of her destination the dog explained she was aware of nothing she was unaware of how her protrusions might scar. The dog bit her epidermis she whipped back toward flange fell on it biting with her underteeth this time.

THE THUNDEROUS MOUTH STACK
For they had inland, other settlements, faces tendril cupped looking for material to shape into answers. Always a scene, a walk, a door. He speaks she speaks *it isn't as though adding the s to experience will automatically entitle you* not as though the regimens won't go on regardless *the little café on the corner* of your current attitudes is open all the time, breaks and starts with countless eggs, yum yum, occasional religions assembling, the periodic devourment we call lunch itself knock-kneed like loud-voiced men in the middle she is stopped and looks around at no one there, the bread half-way to her cheek, she licks her mouth she brushes the bread gently the airy sponginess touch reminds her.

[GIRL'S SENSATIONS ARE MNEMONIC, TRANSLATION]

SIX
[KANGAROO]

DIDEROT

She'd done it. One hundred and fifty eight miles later Girl slumps in place habitually as though book minds made her a gift to exchange this year, because everyone was sure to forgo history anyway, everyone knew the one who died so quietly no one heard, would have sighed in exquisite finality and the sound left quiet to reach eventual ears who're sad that they had living of their own and could not save mortality from itself. That is what the animal counts on *as in the turn toward you and you lash around*, on land and sea and as in heaven's clubbed unknown.

Perfected visitation has its brief to tell her hands moving slowly on the leafy bedspread. Tailored once to fit that bed *we weighted more than once with clay* to see how bodily impressions worked upon it. She and he heaped clay upon the bed, to see how bodies worked upon that surface. *It is not sad or we would laugh amazed, some kind of research on the environment transmitted in that laugh,* a cogitation on the case that every spot of earth has had an accident, the congress of elements in that locale telling you its accidents. In one of her shaking symmetries Girl was trembling to realize this, an *ass-backward* triumph of the invested will.

A precious two or three books she leaned to, having retained them under the tree, in the tent, in her sack, far enough away, a few places to map

[OCEAN DISPERSES EVENT TRACE MORE SWIFTLY THAN LAND]

out, saving them for "later" breaches of time. It wasn't their messages but her reading that located her.

PROPERTY
She nor had nor would know what to do with; the signalman was a property with grist the cats with kittens, the plucked chicken on the table was, the children for whom those responsible, the malleable cornice getting cement set, the open doors of the shops with clothing protruding on steel streamers, the back door with promissory passes those were. Humans liked talk as though words were chemical transmissions, needing the packaging. Flowers bent toward things and leaves held up their parts of the air.

Girl exchanged conversation with total focus on the product, with the proprietor who was a strain upon her torso.
She heard with a definite sense of there being a vacant spot in the purchase of her time since she made no plans, the curvature would do that for her. The curve's an open door.
The "nation" was a battle axe, a sharp set of shared edges. People hummed in caparison.

HUM
The very quiet air from stirring. She had slung her inner tree with string on which her bag and oil and bread. Not a careful meeting she could avoid. Someone wanting to talk to her, to establish.

Girl needing to construct a correspondent set of dream structures to explain the many thread bridges over which to pass was neurological. Though she certainly felt like love but in the medial sense, the little holes for breathing opening and closing, her skin a weather that permits her. She licks her arm and sucks the blood as a reminder.

[OCEAN DOES NOT HOLD ON TO THINGS FOR LATER]

The discovery of sorrow. Hhhh. Her arm with a bandage keeping in the cool keeping in someone treading out desire streams to avoid.

If I don't eat, if I don't eat, the vibrations from my pores begin to shock me, I must shock myself to make the ramped-up holes wider and wider, the tongues of water start to lick me hotly sure I am just about to take them from opening to opening, from mouth to mouth.

BELIEVE IN

The pale wall with curlicues embedded in the cloth, the pale face with grim crept solace temporarily passing, the man with a warm smile urging his chemicals. She could imagine that. Girl checked the little holes for breathing, having no need to make immediately new plans again because of the negative ecstatic situation she was framed in. She had acquired an embroidered sack with elements that tossed softly against her back, she sometimes held hands with a being who set aside her dampness or set against it with its own the little holes for breathing not on purer will.

Boxes in which people prostrate themselves to imbibe and extrude, breathing set in the context of co-breathing, understanding as hello. She wished finally to have that circumstance held close and wandered up to the bar in a line, the intense blue of his wrap lined carefully as a glass spin around his waist – to comfort against the chill? To show someone an apparently changing wind? She held the glass without breaking it and talked.

FLYING CAR DEATH MARCH

Girl was in the car being driven by someone else and the cream-colored large car came spinning out behind them end over end, immediately simulacrum her neck was all around shouldn't they stop *everyone dies it's just a question of when* there's the car they are keeping going, the lecture

[SKIN, WALLS, AND SACKS CONTAIN RELEASE]

on death and the property of the dead the incredible tenderness of the actual she wrote, the labels behind the speaker giving his property away. *We are not a species don't you get that. I mean we don't think that way.*

Later in the building under her feet she felt some softly padded earth on top of which steel rods concrete wood plastic tubing pipes batting thin floors liner carpet, hushing her feet. Getting closer to voices, echo, accumulated noise.

In the city, trains cars buses bicycles shoes legs arms windows shops buildings wires doors clothes; covers motions huffs bleats talk laughs paper blips ticks lights circles squares rough fan particles shafts dun splints wind cable piping setting; noises ground in silts of rocks bone sand glass gems buried water. Your attention could be replaced by solid planning, by the thick visual planes and carping pointers.

She's almost lapsed, she's target normalcy strain hum, she's individuated in the pack feeling the air holds noticing the really altered sensation of hours, almost liking because to recognize the exchange procreations called talking that with their mouths they linger, as in building or arriving or achieving, liking the willing tenuous suspension of loop perception, the air brings people far away from circulation, they substitute apperception with affectionate repetition and she's starting to like that.

TOWN CRIER

She uncovers tears inside her she manifests a crier all alone she is not with a program but lamenting the town she had to leave. A basket now, serviette stall and plain weaving, reading *Geraldine of the Passions*, organizers all cooing birds, deserted rail station at 8 p.m., a man walking with some idea of what's next, someone who means well with teeth in the

[CONNECTION IS THE BEGINNING OF ACTS]

alley of circular progress, tickets as a replacement for fantasy. The cold way out for a fly perched on the book in her hands, he told her *we have a dream of rescue from our lives* what does that mean.

A stranger comes in to smile without reason wants to tell his story he doesn't work but knows his life is good with sharpness pleasure bid more fair more beautiful magnet more a chance than act exceeding age. More death too fine.

He leans and lovely smiles his eyes and posture exceedingly as not having to give ideas more direct than softly hollowed grid, as instruments fair play entanglements, as runaway gambit silver hair more gracious than revealed. *As though the gods were real tomatoes alveolar!* The air huffs pleased out of his mouth.

The laughter of a will gone fabula, temperate as though immense could give her something solidly he asked the flowers all over his face veils walls perfume.

Her head swells like candy.
Your stories charm me out.

Without sin or promises the jeans hold up finer than syringes grace as allocations inside guests, soft and yielded like fat dreams no one remembers without relation comes the train.

CONVERSE
So Girl didn't have to leave the town for now. The little holes for breathing hiccuped stanched. She learned to temporarily domesticate with Gloss.
In your times and my times
he'd say, replete forms and in aches removed from lacking water and

[THE KIOSK JOB CAN'T HOLD HER LONG. PEOPLE LAUNCH OUT OF THEMSELVES TOWARD OTHERS] the leaning feet from the floor, wanting to know, strong force turning up the flue to get the fire to take the hex floating to his flat thin float toward the casters, as though flame shepherds wielded. She started back invisibly, wanting to dovetail.

The sofa has a soft red cover. How to be somewhere exactly names and place names down. *Black coffee please* in the same serpentine labor? Fancy what you stand for, peaks of measure *thank you.*
Pay up fair decent sense of timing two things laughing from the end of the stick. *I love a broken what the track unyielding.*

They were gently hiking in the gentle park. *First time in these things,* old oak, broken waters, false fronts blanking the lease not having to find but give pleasure she having two. Her body thick the core a heavy zone in which his sense could linger though she wouldn't give the torso lodge a name yet, not name its secretions its tiny pressure not leak the secret not as yet. She was waiting to be sure about she knew not what. Maybe an earth chemical would line up its directions?
This is a lovely walk with you. Stay here stay a while the dank hopping furies gave this place its name *not so very long ago.*

POSTCARD
Portrayed as sulky excommunicated hair riding up like curly fountains one man's pyramid on fire he's *explain it.* Folded and attached. *In the finer sense of things the elephant the kangaroo and the horse are all alike trying at some constant final chance, pockets of the stirruped waiting crazy in the building a little like a barn a little like a place deleted.* The flippant sound track kept the barricades in a permanent relation to the horror that became boring eventually, the state whose flagship was her borrowed clothes. How that lingo got in touch with the papers is a miracle to history or her own intact body might easily tell his queries to set down, make midgets of

[GIRL WITH GLOSS: A DESCRIPTION OF PLEASED RELATION]

yourself, tell the screen to burn its hysterical mortal laughter from the wires and ourselves *have done.*

Is that enough explaining do you need something activated for you, are you listening with something other than yourself attending do you pay attention, do you want to "actualize" in some form other than that one doing your bidding now. An admixture of siphoned-off cells, rough lick doing that work. The skin is semi-permanent and you execute a history of brevity, listening to another pull his narrative threads out of his brain and show them to you repetitive beginning at the mirror end.

AT THE MUSEUM

Girl decided colors in art are wet no matter what, though black or white or grey are stone and air and earth. Blue and red clay are water. Not wanting to rid dissent but traveling through investment or speculation on idea by way of his cormorant pale face smiling.
Her new friend Gloss agreed without understanding over green tea.
She quickly smells the chemical trails people follow they choose a little stream and breathe it through. When she crosses against one, major and then minor agitations, minuets of chemical fury.

Late that night in the middle, Girl came back to the museum building and put her arms around it slowly, she got up after a few hours of sleep to go there.
She stood close to the cool warmth of the stone wall, she pushes out her particles and though they are tired hundreds of them unfold and touch.
She spreads her arms wide and holds the tips of her fingers on her left hand tight then shifts herself left and spreads again.
She measured the whole building with the width of her embraces and counted two hundred and thirty-seven spans with arms spread, if someone had stopped she was planning to hold her purple dress fold in her mouth and say *bodily measurement is a new architecture*

[BODIES COEXTEND IN PARTICLE ARTS AND BUILDINGS]

we're planning to average us, to
make way. I am doing a study in which I measure everything with the spread of my
arms. Incredible transmutation of the intellect into enfolding, like eating
the air and folding it back in toward an idea, clasp.
But no one saw her, she didn't have to speak.

TOUCHPAD
Girl looks up as a definition comes into the room. She holds it tangibly
in the morning light, no recession, someone has believed her and put
something aside for her this time, more than a lovely shell. The boy
messenger sits welcomed at the table and eats shuffled cards made out
of chocolate, her latest thing. Like vegetable blood coagulate to artifice.
The wind blows lovingly on the trees, no yearning at all,
it pleasures the room to have you sit.

She works on her presence out of the corner of her eyes the dancing
visitor with fierce icing mellow in the edges. His face is like a cake she
has decided. He gets back on his bicycle with the bag. She keeps a log.
The breasts or the internet are famous they have isolated your touch, the onus in a
certain direction. The cake is "delicious."

THE TYPOLOGY OF ROMANCE
They got into position in the same way every time, his frilly face up
against her little holes for breathing, holding her arms. He was
pernicious on the cloth, convenient purification signaled with boots,
the car embroidered on the spot. He gave himself to the former tenant's
breakfast with a gusto she had felt herself some time back. Skinny with
extruded paradigms, all his ideas forfeited themselves as soon as they
came into contact.

[SOMEONE IS YOUNGER THAN GIRL]

At the park, the birds hopped round forgetfully from the horn blowing too near when they set the car in place. A darling plum. Feet solid on the grass, happy to have been forgotten, she asks her teeth whether they miss coral, she runs her hand darkly on her book, she balances on the consideration of growth and movement, she bites her tongue and felt the thick extrusion of blood. She hurts her answer.

GARDEN

The situation of having to coordinate with others.
That's a sculpture we could agree about, baby-faced and enormous in the heart. A treasure of hawking, simple score card thrashing back and forth amazing as the water's curling fabric, as win. Does she count as a *person?* What's the conversion rate?

Less is sport, *you know, the horizon is lucky light* either way you load it, adjustment wonderful bending turns the flag part when we wheel ourselves around it as *we shouldn't, it says.* Please do not touch.
The party was lovely, an occasion. A brave sun will come around again, don't take it too hard. I'll show you another one she said *I'd be a marvel on that, a choke, tall as houses before the promise,* I promise you.

TENT

It didn't take long. Girl went to the tent with Her, hovered in the sweet dark alone giant rescue air tides almost scrambling. The rustle of soft machinery around her tweet tweet, whoo whoo machinery in her head. Hhhhh. She met her hands gently around her belly. The surfaces responding to the little holes for breathing, folded around an enclosed self she could not squander within a short period, a quiet afternoon. The blue pads, the red ones were semi-permanent, she striking with little hits and Her wielding.

[FOR THE THIRD TIME, GIRL TASTES HER BLOOD]

MISSION

It sucks in this place for a repeated job, a circus with mercy, with a dog instead of rare animals, with pipes that played, with smiling rotundity and an amused gusto, a man speaking loudly and charming everyone.

Their rarely used car had stopped on the road outside town. Too far for groceries, the nibbly greens. They stood watching the children at the table looking unemplaced but feeding, those pushed off the table looking toward the window by way of don't look up, the fovea of the eyes. She got a bowl and loving them sat feeding.

Girl is spelling again, a group at the bookstore, murmurs in her sleep, gratitude gratitude, she's against the tent on the inside, she's on the thin mattress spell. She's in the morning talking, talking again she is evanescent or vanishing, vanquished, she is vacant vacuous vacillated. She spells things for passersby: nutrient gradation implacable incongruous bale.

She deranges a salon, she sets up an umbrella to sell candies, she encourages hats. At the café the computer says Her hometown is full of rain, her books are full of anthropology. The computer becomes an answerer to Girl's well-being, turn it toward others, transitional, transit. In this movement she finds Her at home. So literacy becomes her and loquacious, open.

ROOST

Now, speaking incessantly to her womb in a murmur we can't hear, Girl turns ideas into electric cells with hum. She encourages her shell gland to divulgence, since time isn't real and propagation can be self-inspired time-delayed. That trigger point as though internal bends rise up to meet

[GIRL GOES OFF WITH HER. SHE TAKES A JOB IN AN ETHICAL CIRCUS]

you, to which she adds the sweat glands of those standing near enough to get close, a kind of chemical relation achieving optimal dimension as though you get pregnant by just looking at someone. Her body chose the sea. A wail drives through her and becomes the tender walls, her skin a breach between, and the internal one has hit the ground at last.

Afterward, she got in the habit of fabric and paper.

[AFTER COMPUTER IMAGING, GIRL SELF-CONCEIVES]

SEVEN
[HER]

CRISIS
Dear we've paid the green receptacles we've gleaned emotion Gloss sent our way,
not too bad, not too daring beseeching the candy – the particles through the air
breach her face's kind cement against experience, the blue walls she shut
out post haste venture streaming – these are refutations, collaborative
healing events also known as cultural intervention,
those early times when your own leaves stick out your ears and fingers, traits for
syllabic surfaces,
someone who will be there and someone who really wants to be in this
state forever or who really wants to stay in a boat fixed in banded light
for whom drops every western solidarity into a fine-boned timber shack.

A lightly heaving model sits beside her on the seat of someone else's car,
her eyes make salt water she licks and moves aside with her hands like
animate bones. So Girl learns how deep the match goes, how quick the
timbres splinter wet with land commands. The issue of recurrence and
discrete events, how different, how invincible. Getting at the relation
between what one desires and what forms rise up to toggle. Who is this
one and does she.

Girl had never been in a solely female group like this one, warm and
vacating, streaming at the same time. The air open, light sweat and

[MORE OF GIRL'S INNER EXPERIENCE OF HUMAN RELATIONS]

85

cream, *hhhh*, tendrils reach around her the long hair floats in the car, the softer faces and wide eyes water breath in questing push the alchemical toward her little holes for breathing.

The combination of the next instance its own newness. *You want an answer to that or is it a question telling the story of its pose?* It turns out she doesn't want an answer so much as continuing question, the teeth of the mind engaged in the act of chewing, which is generalized positivity yes. *Hand it back and forth, watch the wafers cluster in a floating accommodation.* The wafers are the sentences, they lightly crunch. Yes, you are not a "type" or a group, we are the singleness the vex point strewn with the particular, anatomy in-clustering. "I don't know."

RASPBERRIES

The island was still though the river went around it. White green brown and red tenders. She set up her gear against a bush. For the next hour she ravages that small island of its raspberries, looking up every now and then for bears and men with guns as she had been told. *Her rags were riches.* The tent was blankets made of tissues. She wipes herself with them carefully afterward and the next morning. It was a long walk on the stony road, her net bag hovering brushing her side, the gentle flies occasionally visiting.

VITA NUOVA

She took off her coat she took off her hat and led her into occupied Asia, they shared a table and chair the greens of swarthy staying. They said bon courage, Girl thought of islands practicing bumping against them low down in the water, the medial dark saline moving slowly up toward the surface and if not transcendence can the social self dispose constraints for one's whole ontology? Is there an identikit defibrillator here, in this café? *Can you electric float with me there too?*

[THESE WOMEN HELP HER PORES THINK]

Her skin lifted off delicately and sifted ions parallel to where she waited, her hair fell up her eyebrows arced to where the black and white photographer might capture them, her stance unwielding possible future time of letting others in the commentaries, textual diffusions she'd meant to understand as grown on gentle curls
I can show you where they say that I can point out the particular place in the paradigm come and see.

Girl fostered an idea of pushing down into the ground, slow drilling like maybe you could find water there too; maybe the holding of a human body was an earth hold; maybe the wet frame's management was fickle in a good way; maybe that was the start of contrast between vertical and horizontal that was conceptual, though pressure obtains whenever she moves up and down.
The replacement of one body by another but with regard, the differential chemicals of this one electrifying her at a low level speakingly, the similar trajectory of obeyed resilience and living cells pulsing disguised as culture.
Her mouth it moves distinctly, tongue and soft inner of the cheeks, glottis, palate, *talk.*
Her pushed flesh dully soft inside her mouthing, sucking it and fleeced with holding, her palms a little rough the art the stitches from the cuts against the grass. If I could have held you up inside the delicate city.

GENUFLECTION
Later I'm at a film-work playing light on her face, a parable of ash until it's replicated. An old film treated in its physical form.

No stand this way and the light will swoon on that strange-colored skin you've got.

Like this.

[THEY COMPARE LAND AND WATER LIFE]

Yes well partly more toward the window, to capture the tints – they look like bruises made three days ago, that's what they're like!

The sound of buildings falling on the themes of Girl's arrival by the glass *or anyway that's how I saw it.* How they plague her eyes somewhat as yesterday sitting on the front porch of Her city, not so surprised after all this time to be performative with unconscionable reason, Girl did talk. Her lips formed shapes transmission while the cars floated near in the *beloved community.*

All afternoon they sat together watching the instrument cages develop on the serious side of cult animation, the movies paralleling the increments *a citizen might come to take as their life, time thus scored as real, clothes moving from one person to the next, the hapless visitor quite random in biological form now*?

The person Her was nowhere near like vagabond or silly, her frames locale enlarge. Like air might parallel the former life, might give permission to some at least who might then make it spread.

Girl found her face smiling, the interlace supportive of the little holes for breathing, a conversation entered and an airstream folding in and through, Her getting closer and the belly slowly surged.
Hhhh
they can always find you smiling
she makes designs for the novice tread of skin, the soft bird fluttering down from the sky towards her instinct
it'll take years, my darling, years before you sort this out marine promise, the movement of a tin-shaped fire dashed into parts, the possibility of some juncture Girl was finding quite amazed. The woman's face was arced in black and grey and pale, like the depth below the water line far enough

[HER PHOTOGRAPHS GIRL. THEY WATCH FILMS TOGETHER AFTER]

to vanish color, the woman's face clear on the screen in glowed ascendancy though petitioning, begging, ready to do anything.

Bag

That time at the doctor's, Girl held a mirror between her legs at her speculumed vagina so she could see the cervix, which looks like the wet tip of an uncircumcised penis slipped out into the shone light, like a succulent anemone pulsing. An eyepoint right in the middle, deep color around the look. A bag a sac a particle, a soft resistance plummeted, a strain you're held down by.
Yes it's true, the regulations are specific in this regard.

That's the edge on which her feet skirt, tinted mammal suckling in slow degrees via the oceanic syllables, mama mama, take me to the windstorm of your daddy mind, take me with you the unpeeled navigation of the immediate aftermath being where did she? Floating afterward to the sounds of that guitar. *Years is whats I don't have but so there.*

Honestly

Girl shook herself out of her blankets wary of the tuck. She embraces the book she'd been carrying ever since the campsite, never clear on *how* it functioned *for* but comfortable now with the idea of carrying things, how visible and invisible accumulate differently in relation to your body as you hold a culture to you in the water, in the air.

Birds were allocated to the woody things and the windows gave place for smaller buzz while she made her morning tea. She had found a place, her legs were firm and this Her was love by deal. The lance between the interior echo and the pain in the moving legs was the degree to which she was prepared to have the trip out totally.

[HER ACTS WITH TIME. GIRL, PREGNANT, DOESN'T SAY]

Design studios need some assistance and Girl was happy to help shapes achieve new form, happy to work tangentially, to ascribe ideas to anyone, flip out and the measurements cloth, chairs, drapes, human clothing, it was amenable.

Her skin is tethered the wet bones sulky glisten in the half-dark she would stay a while, the ticking arbitration of the agreement she had made with the memory of her mother.

VOLUNTARY
Her outside legs were dry, her eyes fixed on the cloth touching. Someone told her to do something, take that measurement, what do you think. The continuity was creeping, the asseverance. The knowledge outside herself was a kind of relief.

In the night Girl lay doubled. On one side the sound of an animal on the other the cool cloth of the sheet.
The darkness was slate and red, her torso holding soft organs silting waves of tiny magnetized parts whose processing required subtle diminutions and pulse, the rays moving like a harbor seal, the tiny portions quickened by the moon of the head pulling on the blood waves. True that collision streams were ambient crossing neural love patterns reaching fortitude unsealed: the individuated mass finds bound the filters and repair the soothing invisibility, the eyes closed arms shifting with moving the torso one side and another to optimize how your body occupies in the pressure of air and ground.
The body emanates salt perfumes, tiny reeking.
She turns on the soft light gets the encyclopedia images and begins naming her parts: Sisyphus Amanda regicide wisdom serpent clam pennyroyal bread Roland wingspan commoner fence.

[NIGHT-TIME REVERIE]

THERE ARE NO OPPOSITES
Girl was finding out, the sack over her shoulder and that brilliant
possibility from shining...
the tender shapes with names had not abandoned her. She held the
outline of the idea of its continuance in her arms sometimes, licking the
roseate nipples and licking the tender vulva, pushing her tongue into
the pores one at a time or they would walk through the forest together
showing... she slept with an arm over her breast, the sheets bowing on
either side....
when the air is wind it's like water/home/breath?, the tracheotomy rouge
continually, the little holes for breathing animate...

EXCHANGE
Fortunately, art had prepared them both, though in different ways.
To investigate the ratio for behavior to sad-sack the wishy-washy to
ready the armada to be kind – Girl was learning. She needed thus to
explain, to *have it out* without turning away.

The trees were smiling indulgently as she prepares in a walk. She
returns and tells Her splendid stony softened, the real touchpad inked in
the turn.
*Because the information with material approaches grief or spent regionalism, all
at once and constantly, the rivers the water places concurrent and life bled? Like the
land inverts that quarry in the hidden places where animals sit and have neither
visible nor not visible but position, posture, aiming at and aimed?*

Questions were replacement parts like rungs, one slatted in the turret
another in the eyes, the movement of the air while the lungs intook and
secret. The standing rice paper screen while she inveigles her pajamas.

[GIRL WRITES FOR HER PHOTOGRAPHS]

The pushing together of the breasts, nipples meeting soft and lips, the skins turn inside out over each other, lips to lips and the raspy tongue opening the water of the brain. She was hungry the warm water strewn with salt and thick, thick with eating. The dense grey of the water turned her head from side to side, then as now in operation glistening.

What it means to mean to do something with your own and someone else's body. Love's little deaths like bone sighs down her throat. You take in the world it takes you in and you take it, and you give it out pay out and yield. There were significant slides between her ability to see things the way others might construe them, and certainly it was never about pain but acts that cut across continual. As in "the news" where people and other animals always die.

Broken typo on the greensward, she typed it again: broken typo, the keyboard spelling backward she was typing on the keyboard detached from power sources with the abbreviated machine leant to her, the broken apparatus of a body in keeping with the movement of the match, the defenestrated body whose openings are clear to view, the spilling out of the instance of salt water there the licking and plain seeing.

IN A CAFÉ
Girl sat ready by the next person she was getting to know, *how do you do*, where are you from, what do you do to situate yourself, when you are meeting strangers how do you keep yourself from plunging headlong toward the plan you have already set in your heart, how do you retain that tethered slowness, that press-against-you energy to apply yourself directly to the listening stranger
how do you do
you retain the energy to get up and not simply turn to the task you have set yourself. Circles inside circles abounding.

[GIRL LOVES HER TO DEATH]

But what question is she asking and which is she being asked?, did he
plan to save that bit of sandwich for her or did he simply leave it next to
the piano in the event? Hard to say, she wrote on the disconnected item
she had carried with her into the forest that day the trees were keeping
themselves company and not seeing her at all despite the great scene with
the talking ones who threw things at the girl, they weren't very powerful
and so couldn't have done any real harm kind of like an individual life it
has to be connected to some other power units to do any real harm
are you listening to me are you
devoting yourself to keeping hard back from the curve that is ready to
send you over toward the rolling edge of this land mass toward the plan
you maybe set?

MERMAID'S PURSE
*Out of which will come my divine friend, the child of my assailer, the assizer of my
plans, the ecstatic potential machine, the wind in the water, the torrent of mercy,
the breakage in my brain*, the potential non-meeting of the object Girl has
become these many months on land and the object she remains and
the fatalism of the circumstance of her agglomeration to this pseudo-
memorial to the moment of inception. She'll go back, she won't go back,
the circumstance of her idea having arisen in that barque of the body the
long tomb somebody plans to revisit once she has readied herself; she has
met the land, that claimant of dry readiness and borrowing to that ship
over the edge has sailed to – *what do you mean*, ready?

MENTAL BREAKFAST
He'd like to take up archery and the violin, he said he wanted to script
a whole culture to be performed in a single day, he showed me how his
land language gave him permit like a drug, several pieces of identity
paper he showed when he introduced himself to new circumstances,

[GIRL IS BACK IN THE FOREST. HER QUEST BODY REPLACES HER]

summed up in one promissory note and backed by many external witnesses.

How you been baby, on this here journey
to be voicing combinations of what might laugh when
serious incarnate cruelties defined themselves according to their hampering of desired conditions he said

We laughed and shared the innards of tortured birds he laughed and we pressed the grapes and turned the bread to water he laughed with his whole body he was protected for amazement.

He said not a time a place can eat you slowly the gentle smile of the long world becomes sovereign, incapacitated by attention
he said scary and nice in the wind and rain his eyes shining his face warm and young he held his ideas up to the window of silver and history, the year the wall skinned happiness to Girl, who thought a layering effect would make the net pliable, negotiable, Ramsey was in the photograph tucked in the book, was this always his name, he was in the other room fresh ardors.

He wants to replace himself, he insists like desire can make something happen. He is her landed fornicator he has ideas and returns.

Girl has the biscuit on her tongue and counts the forelocks that shake out from the paddock soft were sleeping her once skated head could fall the petals fast again.

An animal story *by the road the man insisted on taking the land by mouth and staging it to completion*, his large metal plates succored permanent by entrails coupled walks.

(He is back again.) Some kind of mannered selfhood set there on the brooding see and made her country spree inveigle all her looks.

[GIRL'S EVENTS ARE SIMULTANEOUS . . .]

Aquarium slice. *Because the story happens at once, you know all that, it's entirely arrived in the cut across the source code of the wreck, in the shoulders holding themselves while the country wails its placards as the animals cut each other with meaning.* She keeps finding him through other parts of stories that leave themselves behind.

Her eyes were deeper, her hair dry as ivory, the book under her hands rife with thoughtful admonitions and hope patterns, its dark swirling cover slightly pudgy excrescence seeping very slowly to her fingers and thence to her brain. She thinks watching the animal crowd we're waiting dealing sidelong cards, who laugh at whose, who are preyed to fetch, who hire someone else to care.

DECREPITUDE
In a side park in the middle of a day, Girl was practicing time near the aquarium, calibrating with her skin and holding her torso, and *like* were people translucent could you *see right through them* to their invisible deaths? She watches an old woman cross the grass. The woman moved with care like a crab or a very young kitten, aware of the tendrils and shoots of the grass along the sightlines of her musculature and bones and skin. Girl had taken off her shoes for it was a warm day close to the river. The old woman concentrated on her motions then stopped and looked up at what was ahead, turned to the side to look, then continued her deliberate walk. Inside the old woman Girl hears the blood move gently like a slow water surge and abeyance, the electric field perfused with ambient recall patterns of plan the gathering particulars brushed up along the fact that this had happened and that had happened. Thus moods and contorted expressions shape her face and movements like leaves inside her whoosh. The grass was loud on her. Was it sound or triumph or what arrow that shed the skin of those you look at? Girl puts her eyes outside of her and they look up very far high and in very close.

[. . . WASHED BY CHEMICAL MEMORY]

95

RECALL

Hello is the third person in the very large room, it must have happened
when she was sleeping, that was the time when he, when the teacher
must have done, that was the certainty that preordained that moment in
recovery later when she was no longer a tangent to her own body, her
mother an expulsion of relief, expurgated of love, vile though the thought
had been of an absence of something prevenient, suffering that made
the recall potent and negotiable, the child made of stroking fur, after all
she would move away, had gone away, and the thickening rounded body
becoming –

The moment the sassy person began her suit Girl was balanced in the
precipice of worry, that she would not again be able to – not to be able
to experience, to forestall – not be able to honestly make that transition
again – it was liminal in the way she had learned that instant phrase like
a coating on the body, *pathos*, "like an invention to keep you from owning
your own suit if you see what I mean," the clothes splayed out like a blue
club on fire, the dark wet immolation necessary to the point of view she
was trying to set up without promises to herself or here nor anyone.

She wedges her fingers along her blue arm, the nostalgia for wet
pressured darkness the imbued layer gland keeping her eyes wet.
She told him about her *special viviparity*, that she'd turned her body
sideways and squeezed her inner shell from side to side, a slow push of
sense, *okay, we'll take this one we'll take her*, her own self agrees fruition's
motile turn. She is already honey with blue vegetables. That's all right,
whose turn comes along.
She can hold the seed then put it in herself, you know. The palette honey
wooden paint job closing up the shop of the body seals it off.
This garnet light, I'm wearing it fully inside, it's all now glow.

That's okay. I'm good with that.

[GIRL TELLS THE SASSY MAN SHE'S IN SEED]

When you don't see someone anymore that's when they have died, or died to you.

THE GLASS FACTORY
Blueberries with blank hearts included, she left these at the doorstep they provide for him, ambitious footsteps here flet out, there spleening for the new one tucked under an arms.

Solicitude has designs like those on cloth that flutter in front of her eyes at night, more dire need for designs some torpid some frenzied some flash what the co-worker calls old man with cramps needing certification, you get closer to opaque significance, you roll over on the covers. Like the waters, the airs full of repeating, needing to repeat, needing to tell yourself never enough to say it only once. Her smiles with extremely temporary wisdom over the ice cream. Girl noses up her novice, instinct salt.

That's a blue skull she thought
I'll wait for the fine shine light through glass enclosures nothing there's
she turns her head and the blue light cuts right through material method cannot be indifferent to the blue glass where folds of her belonging (whether or not held) provide a similar sense sought that open door she shifts beside her wanting represented by a full blown stretch of blue sky blare beside the wasted playground both nearly old and nearly new wreathed in her purple eyes. Glass blown into air streams fitted in frames.

Without talk her interior becomes completely available, where anything can happen. Maybe that's the reason crystalline of desert shining flatly in the long-range wrapped-up pipes all the way to city plans —

[GIRL'S GLASS FACTORY JOB. THIS HAPPENED EARLIER, HENCE THE BLUE GLASS ON HER PHOTOGRAPHS]

maybe that's the light she's growing toward while

you smile and stamp your feet at all the mysteries that happen with these names attached. Glass depending thinly in her fingers

Hillbilly icicles, that's what we call these sellers. Take one home and put it by your door!

[MUTE POSSIBILITY]

EIGHT
[PEARL]

PHOENIX

I sat beside an animal on my way it soothed me with its bloody paradigms I made three lists: what to do with people she had gotten to know, what to do with the broken ones, and what to say.

Her content ledger fettered the soft blue aligning sky into permeable membranes whose wet quotient was tangible, but far away she was there is a witness. The animal looks at her insides, hhhh.

A spark made the lights pretend electric spire smoothed down romantic solicitude: the building with burning, are all those windows broken are they open, is the water safe or eyes made dull, are there children inside the auction patches on their arms, made for animals to taste the risk, they can never be sad or dull or hemispheric, her personal confab soothes the lilac wallpaper plasticizing the edges of the broken windows animals adhere to, why save them from the information they must confront at last, their rivulets as ready for the torrents now as later, with an altered shape and set of *promises to self.*

SHRAPNEL

Deterministic blooms on toast, the jam as blueberry advent. Girl's mouth fills with the ritual event of teeth and tongue and items getting in the way that need to go down. Each time she tells a story another bunch

[GIRL STUDIES ABANDONED BUILDINGS]

emerge, like tandem queens they wave, like water berries. Girl is delighted, she feints. The stories blanch and fake, they posit adventure as a substrate. Where are you from where are you *from*. The crunching fruits inside her tongue her teeth she chomps the yielding part the dominant body surge. Her teeth are pearled coral with diadems mushed on her tongue, her eyes are introverted delicate to the taste. Yum yum.

Pearls
She is a shiny delicate subclass, a supernumerary arm candy, she is demitasse and serving spoon, she peals. A dish of coffee ice cream with cherries smeared all in.

You are so beautiful.

Yes, I've heard. But I don't mean, I mean –

It's hard to explain. In the event of a pointless or pointed departure, she would always have a story for the next round, something to placate that version. Pedetic, star-bloom. She was on her way and as you will, she told Ramsey this as soon as they met she told Gloss she told Her, she tells the adventitious as soon as she pulls her sodden body out of the waves in curiosity. She wouldn't need to mention that, wouldn't need to have told you but for the seepage, the tremendous sympathy for fronds and rivers. It isn't so very different from the earth and sky, just mercurial, eviscerated, pell-mell, visible, transmission-hot, suffused, percolating, sound-arced, given to constant touch, to squiggles in the current, to wiggles of the legs and arms their separate ascendancy pushing back together, to portions wherein you look with all the eyes in your skin and portions for the rocks and hidden constants.
Not gone, not gone. He was not the interest, he needed to please out of the way.

[THE LANGUAGE SHE'S LEARNED DOES NOT STOP MEANING]

Plate glass questions keep the walls awash with parlay from this side
the doors hum patiently with eminent cars dovetailed with congregants
temperately *the hotels are sweet to us the banks will give you passage our futures
are crop-worthy children green*
our wild animals will devour us only if we let them
*— tell me how your study of idea is proceeding, or if you've got distracted by your
accurate friend sitting there with baskets full of ripe fruit* — and all the stone
angels slavering around the park their faces washed with sticky fumes
the eyes roiling blank glee. The park's shot through with tumid cluster
tree seed trails, it's hunkered afterglow.

Yes, like innuendo, I've studied about that.

A car glares its human eyes in line. The building fat with excess
anatomical weight, the bodies roll inside. Girl turns back to the
sidewalk, time for lunch.

WARDROBE
A smiling cat on the walk, or grimacing, the crusty grin splayed tight
against its cheeks, the off-white teeth pared promising, the forelegs
tufting out the fur so pretty cadmium chisels the invented monk-like
posture the weird calibrations of its eyeballs the sunken ranges of cloth
magnets like dust bombs cloaked along the sides the hind legs tending
backward toward the tree edge the figurated gauze ground down to
stone mound packed the pleasing aromatics of fading screech to stretch
parade, the dry down frisk of sotted limbs like balustrades they hanker,
they wear, they are furball sculpture scrapped as cloth in the plastic:
oh, she thought, it's manded here, it's requisite not floating pieces off in
wet dissembly, it's flat remainder not the given centrifuge of mission in
equilibrating wet. But there is pleasure in the vivid haspics of the left
for dead in the very next painting, very alive in this one.

[PEOPLE GIVE PARTS AND WANT WHOLES]

I don't have aspect birthdays. I don't have continuous calibrations nor flanks at mountain bear or snare drums to the smoldering bridge of near-bleeding. There are so many landed terms I lack.

Girl ponders on this with her wet umbrella singing in the sudden wind, as though keeping her company, kept in find if true. She is wielding the umbrella with her well-developed holding hands that have kept her from falling more than once this time.

Maybe the rain could help to keep the surfaces wet. It could be deployed.

You're funny.

On the way, someone waiting with munificence having given up prior aspects gave them to Girl. *How do you say that, then?*
The world sloughs off clothes from dead children, from the wailing hairs of several gods' misfit traps, half-moon eyes of the person who stays within his other to keep his cultural junction at a misfire when you come, or these bodies you mean to collapse they do collapse, so wetness could preveniently wash all that away I mean could serve. Her minutely fractured limbs go all directions with these clothes, the rough parts of her skin tear anything fine.

Figuring how to thicken her lives, she puts on all the clothes at once: the shirt, the robe, the red dress, the creamy one, yellow pants, blue shorts, the translucent fabric, the skirt, the boots, t-shirt, button-down, the jeans, the scarf, the hat, the ring and gloves, the cape. She stands in the shower. She took the matches to set it all on fire (which didn't work because of the water). She ran stuffed half-thickened to the stream by the artist's house. The clothes all over her wet and flagrant, off.

[HOW MANY LAND ACTS CAN BE PERFORMED AT ONCE?]

MUSIC

A shift, a score, some kind of pipe, a phrase like animal announcement, a plaint rift, things not quite meeting together or rather not quite blending not ensemble exactly more like co-presented. The artist's fabrics are like clouds. Girl likes the art when nobody pretends harmony in the sense of parity or tight weave among the instruments.

Better yet was walking out and several days later among the scrubby bushes where the wind and electric ringing in her head hearers and the sound of her pores and breath and hair rustling and the sound of the branch units shuffling and the theatrics of the sky made little noises it was what Ramsey had absurdly called absolutely quiet. (When they were alone.) Her mouth blocks had rounded into firm sounds she half-sang, half-talked, in acquired set pieces that fit in the postured receptacles of human ears.

In this city they speak additive tongues, their lips curling like clam sides the tongues nitrate and basalt. Girl leans forward to catch bits, her ears enormous shells fill out. She has a pretty idea of that. She adjusts her skirt and pants in the heat. Her skin subtending implements with the rain she'd saved in deeply.

GARDEN PARTY

Four wrens fell to fight it off after one hit the window with a neck-breaking thump, startling everyone. Aquamarine weather, half-way Paston hands careful at work, she who waits who dunced. In books.
Heartbeat music, so you're calm there.
Born here.

Born inside there, the tendril polyps reaching one recognition to another, how we know each other like skank in animals, agreement is like wanting everyone to have the same friends so we can all *stop. Not at all.*

[IS THERE EITHER "SILENCE" OR "SOLITUDE"?]

The seating of the smiling man and children groomed, that unavoidable red lace he drove around with a grave in his truck she walks around with ideas in her hair, little crimp objects. The whole skirt as one removable mystery. *Hhhh, hmmh.* Born as coming out in one locus, the flat land takes the thump and blood inside.

Soap of passersby, darts of income, hatted trumpet, calling *child*, fluff of wind purple umbrella faraway barque feather cigarette spilling *Charlie* ornament cough naught nigh, the creek spur landscape photographed in a murmured query voice walk metal breath air thumping soft whisk *smile crouch with a little step*
he undid all the sweeping up a shuffle really roaring air bare feet yes insistence, gentle interlude.

Long enough to know better. If only I could please avoid a repetition of *that* fate, she said perkily.

Girl smiled, her lips curving out toward the sky, that about does it.

Invisibility wraps itself lovingly around you again, it's the approaches, long and heavy on long and heavy. Their skins all took on the color of dinner. Compound, resembling a spread hand. They have a long conversation across the meadows, she plump and congenital, showing not telling.

Across the darling meadow sounds as holding, snakes and whirring birds. The horses had been put in for the night and she had two more weeks to go on the Traveling Helpers dock sheet. They had to talk about what had happened, what something meant from the long afternoon of one week past. They had read their books in the interim to provide themselves with extended metaphors of potential significance.

[GIRL HAS A JOB WITH ANIMALS WHO AREN'T TRYING TO EAT HER]

I think it means savoring, cloying dissevered into molecules, not that he was cruel but that the customary approach was one we simply do not recognize. Girl nods thoughtful.

A fresh start for Jennifer, that's one way to put it and during the laugh her sensible arteries pulsed with muffled containment.

If I wrote to anyone, where? About five at once might raise their arms and imitate darkness. My feet are on the boards now, another problem to clear the way through.

I have condemned you to life; let me be the face of love for you in that sentence. Mother mother, sharp lines of explanation. Yellow orange dark green peek of illumined transient, mouth opening to smile, in to which a human set extrudes. You walk away from the party.

AQUARIUM
One is no closer whenever it occurs. Can you pick the seeds up can you. The fountain squirting out is like very thin blades beneath her flesh, they sluice downwards, each step a collapse.

Not that she is ever alone, dependent on that distance as we are. She lifts another foot that protrudes as though in invitation a tiny flush of blood suffuses gently into the shoes, held fine within like her organ acid is upheld within her gravity-pressed torso.

One building holding another, building as in receptacle you'd think being in one. Her modeling was the lover in the world of devourment, backwater brewing inside her legs instead of sweet isles, a dirty river on the causeway of her flesh was the hand tracing its asserted right to be there, as though a fish would be distraught that you would want to take its life by treachery! The life in the blank, water blanked on stretch a separation. Hello pretty animal, winged sufferance circling and watery

[GIRL IMAGINES WRITING TO HER MOTHER]

ululation. One must consider the difference between an owned world
and an inhabited one, the glass around your venue air or water, pressure
belts, gravity ties. Where are you when things *come along*?

She walks around the back of the tank, searching for a way in, footsteps
clicking softly. When she became aware of the folds of clothing, the
swish and hold, it was already too late. *You want it you want it hold me you
want it* hold tackle swift, why then "I'll fuck you" tackle swift full
in the sharp holes breathing, the breathing hole and whine down hard
on the floor. Her head swerves with the pelt heave, in an inside her cunt
fronted with his penis in and out the entail limbs held her skin inveigled.
But no, come on.
She brings her underteeth out dermis broke, this shit for skein breaking
in her feet, her thrashed legs hold on the floor again and it's a wet aquatic
floor, an extremity of case broken out, his blood out, another one she'll
do it again, she's got it: the anointed world experienced, full carving
what it's best at hear it, give it, here it is.
This time she really knows what is meant and what she means it back.

Rose
Which might not be seen. What reckoning should she take at this point,
so colored by the sun as you'd imagine? The scales tipped toward a dry
underground point of view? Her simple bag has become boxes trunks
and stars leapt out in casual happiness, cars and trees splayed nearby for
a fee.
*My best asbestos still has to go; it's no longer courteous to do beloveds upright and
half-clasped.*

It's like total golden caves arrayed in bounty hunt, seeming to invert
the original excursus; a person pleasant in his fits although he barely
understood her refusal to add flying to her repertoire. In that economy

[At an aquarium, Girls kills her rapist]

the penis pushes out and the vagina pushes in, the eyes at either end
exchanging see-saw, tidal retribution sworn on the witness stand.

The girl I fancy drives a car (*for now*) with syllables wrapped in her clothes
now twinkling (then)
she turns her nonce further than we'd imagined, men portioned toward
her, the thick air light at the top and heavy where the animals move
around their serious faces.

Pleasant in his fits, limpid in his clothes, gloomy of moon with phrases
that could rout him, the girl next room and wholly of silk or rue before
she woefully careened the car. Every layer of being a carapace blinkered
or strewn. All the lights are on.

My god the testimony is almost irreversible for the blue skull, for the
ornate perfumery she may be the testimony, the variety of options laid
in front of *I don't know rose what would you do here with your virile antiquity and*
everything cut out?

THE HORSES KNEW
The moon is a large elevator circling the sky. Girl becomes a sweet one
given to place, blankly as a tirade, enormous river gathering paper
blanks, journal habitués gently fondling their ideas all around her like
they could take ribbons and attach them to her disappearance.

Testimony: the gathering of information according to arbitration rules.

It's early morning and she's put out the trays. Her dress is only pink.
She keeps packets of salt for sweetener, she makes tides swell on the
enormous referents culture keeps pushing forward in the form of
convenient packages. She builds paper boats and heaves them toward
the hot futurity of dawn.

[SELF-DEFENSE IN A COURT OF LAW]

And when she's made the tea she calls them down, down, holding the warm breads with sound buzzed over the buffet walls, the winds outside the windows stretching out the cars on her convex eyes, trying to image the river in the root beer barrel building up to hold the weight of visitors.

Conversations are islands taken from enormity by night and compressed in crinkly packages, they whoosh into time, into the water-without-sound predominant and suddenly without witness define themselves, here all along. The woman not quite old steps in the same time every day all week.

The horse Girl rides whichever one she chooses pushes up its shoulders when the saddle slumps, when her pelvis clamps around. The sharp skin riding on the bristles, the tremendous wet air rushing out of the nose, those fine hairs delicate and wet and open Girl touches. Their bodies are very clear, large caverns filled in with dark pounding, ready to live.

I help the people who come in wanting a sandwich. Their molecules are tight when they arrive, their eyes tight and seek, they smile with teeth and get a food. They suck and swallow, bite, chew, chew, lick, adapt their noses ears and jaws to the objects they put inside their mouths. It's wonderful, they are fixated in the repast and you pass by slowly and they close up a little, their torsos swing a little, they do not give up, they will look at me cheeks big and they growl in their pores. They swallow and swallow. They shift their torsos waiting for the urine and faeces to formulate for the grub, they smile at a surface and understand each other perfectly. Their teeth stew and simmer. When they pay they are relaxed, their holes open, their ideas wandering, their eyes no longer fixed on my position.

ST MERCY
The young person blind-sided, sterile to environment, grew by edges.

[GIRL TALKS TO A FRIEND WHO'S HELPED HER]

Cars went by faster than experience, so one knew the objects sitting in front of her were positions. The story-teller as a pose, his skin peeled from its tomb embrasures lovely for the nonce.
So we were houses, and I was waiting with that still common voice.

Sure, sure. As birds too, they call them, having met their antecedents, will try anything. Not uncommon, such mickery she was finding. He told her
the straps were not spared as I hitched to response.
That's what bail is for. Not better than the teeth suddenly, she considered. We'll call it double mercy applied to sentences: he bent, she bent, you bent.

They entered the hospital's automatic doors. Benediction, which means it's almost over and he is closer to something he wants, the sky and the knees tucked under her chin. "Wastrel" or "scoundrel" waiting for narrative with open hearts, colloquy rush.

EVERYBODY WAS BEING FAIRLY KIND
Though stringing together the elements of your words, I seem to be missing something.

Delicate appurtenances of self-devolved ideas, small sets of people trial given to understand.

I mean you've told these stories a hundred ways, soft branches slowly over your head, even I heard whispers, expedience, narrow passageways for exiting. But the story went on hour by hour, sticking together the pads of her hands from holding, soft minstrel waiting without form for the woebegone.

[HER FRIEND IS IN THE HOSPITAL]

It's like she is swallowing a long string of tender beads that expand and dislocate inside her and never come out any side again.

Under the sea
Wash day, directive girls on ideas sloped on tables, table people sloped toward one action at a time, sound crescent hits on dye sheets. She knelt herein with a pitch on cloth, missed bats and scrip both in and out ways all trod forth, the mid-scene catastrophic veer, on off again, plinked merely. She reports in regularly, a little better understanding power.

Someone plays while they clean the floor – dove tunes on the sail strings, a wrench slid across for fixing something spent on time
"I lawk around and peer myself serene, ha ha, I hawk and vent some twosome gewgaws split on mouth soft"
(piker not worth two cents given not two ways blent your scenery) she mixes to underwood, his keen spleen split wood parts to beetles.

They climb strenuous pat soft ways – gone leaves little hands covered with scratch marks scrim, soft to going, *I've made peace with your divestment and I'll sit here soft* with padded friends – the growth at my head no battling we, you wait, a kite seen leaving trees like aft we ask it winked like furnishings sweet notched to the pinker deeds – brace you're falling the lads blowing the girlfriend balanced on her toes, up in your eyes, in your nails, your hair in pioneer sunglasses perched.

Honey comb my hair, brush it back with pyramids, doodle stripped lounges on my inked machinery, youth fiery with fire sing your pyre with smile and ifs you
sit there with your parts so fine no more therein than who were mine.

A dressed white knob, a moving tree with water in her dream brain, the arched-back posture of a delusional litigant completely atopic to yielding

[When Girl tries to explain, it's like swallowing. They tell stories instead]

(all right we can understand you as wrong or wrong-headed, your mouth asynchronous with the bestiary we've mottled out...).

Sign here. We're going to prepare your sentence.

THE SENTENCE
All right trying to stay away from human bodies she will paint. Girl will make the sea from underneath the moving rays sent upward through the silt. Her torso looms, arms wrap softly around herself to sleep. Alongside that the slant of armistice, the vibrant steel of truce, like the sky was not *blue* at all. Whose model is the line threaded under her skin, gentle blue under the arm turned brown over out. Canvas made of flesh. Alongside that the series of electric lights bursting with slow shatter, slow implode. Across the lot a friable wrong wet, a disseminated expectation.

She paints enormously: the moon, canvases stretched half the width of the shrink-wrapped room. The canvas is a series of locations she tries again. Her forearms are barely able to make the strokes as thick as she wants. She cuts off her hair to make brushes. She pushes her fingers into her skin to mix the paint with sweat.

Now she needs oils and surfaces, bottles and space. Which meant borrowing, always borrowing the time = space = something *feeling ok* in the value. She is pragmatic in the value, doused in value young in her offices. A relation of exchange whose predicates are not embraced by Girl.

Touching the paint, the dread gorgeous of the wound, purples and ochers for talisman. The fusion machine was hard at work, the comestible exteriors part and parcel of a getting up to make the time what it would otherwise not be.

[SENTENCED TO AVOID INTIMACY, GIRL TURNS TO PAINT]

That person's motto was *staying comfortable making a difference,* but Girl knew half as well a code, a nothing-more then-something, restraint that held her brush flashing at moments of contact. Staccato and smooth, momenting it. The canvas is a skin and oils tattoos, the breaching a dynamite expression she waits to see again from beneath, the disappearance of the whale and reappearance in the rush *awa, stay with me. Ama. Weight the surface with a deep maternal weight, twist in the disseminated aspects of the circling plan.*

She got very good with a stapler gun, with the pieces of wood and tight. It wasn't a plan to give time to the patch of land bordered by roads; but there she went, the inkjet cartridges fallen all over the junkyard where they also collect. Men in suits got out of cars with guns and set up targets after taking off their jackets. Afterwards, men in jeans came round and picked up cartridges for re-loading. In another part of the alternative collective or the dump.

Many objects can be re-collected without plan or sentiment as cloth with smells, kiddie dioramas, bits of carpet, broken chair seats one could stack up for a ladder. Compensation can be made for the far-awayness of the particles as one adjusts to the organisms: Girl took her face close up and painted that, the move from particle to wave. The faceted appearance reduces radar, a surprise involution of what you might expect, and now her torso's second life summons itself in movement, liquid loops. Smiling, she presses in the grindings from her very small fragmenting of things gathered from the dump.

[QUICKENING, HER ART OPENS TO TRASH]

NINE
[TUTOR]

ZOOLOGY

Her keeper has become *most famous* and her turn to move.

I wouldn't want to be apart of that, too watchful for the heartbeat we've unbent.

The soupçons of culture mass not gently against her arms free from pink: thus presents the crow that keeps the man who threw out all the balances, though not unkind. Tripped up, but with her bags and trunk intact. She paints his row of clothes standing upright.

Some barter took her places too. Postcards you couldn't eat, she paints two for people who had given her things she now left behind.

Dear ——————— , I want to let you know the particular shaded shape of ill parsed womens, you know gently arrow gently voice shows your thinking by being different over time. I'm creeping gradually toward immersion awake and fluttering. Thank you for everything you came apart. Gently Girl.

Dear ——————— , the pears are absolutely awake here, "it's amazing" as you said, they nudge their branches green the clouds wake up and take

[GIRL TAKES ART LESSONS AND CORRESPONDS . . .]

113

the light trees lick their leaves with barky tongues; I'm getting it partly on surfaces, partly off, your patrimony like the ground objects you surrounded and then showed me, Girl.

I'LL MAKE MY WAY THICK SHADOWS
Girl spills blue paint all over her arm and worries about toxins and embrasures. She wants to hurry home from the daybed where she trammels canvases and picks apart the threads to affix them, smear colors on top, cut thread and strips of cloth and affix them, stitch through the canvas (but carefully to keep it strong), render the frame multidimensional (instead of always four sides).

She tries to suture in some sound with metal from the dump but that is very hard, it ends up with a gentle twang or tightness *(sznnggg)* she can tune slightly up or down, *and even then we would have to rely on a location where the work could move pretty freely, hang from the ceiling, say, with the possibility of seeing it from the front and back, both sides,* she does it that way. The screws on the back of the frame have the option of being loose or tightened. Her arms are tingling. You can make the piece twang only by a definite involved touch.

The strong pull of the air whose apertures had fallen into themselves, crashed in a swerve, the leaves were like the furnishings they were music like the paintings couldn't bear. Girl has no expectations but the thick swirling of elements around yes. The completely rustled air the high up horizon totally sweepy like pasturelands without defense, she wonders how her skin receives the wind, how the little holes for breathing huff through in relation like the body shuffles inside more than out. Wind is not a spectacle but a thought event, not meaningfully pre-interpreted. *Simultaneity renders her both dead and alive.* It's Gladstone in the air, it's acculturation's resistor. Girl hadn't asked for the trial to be massaged,

[. . . CONSIDERING BOUNDARIES AMIDST ART AND THE BODY]

her *expectations* and her *difference* to be put forward as tangible to seeing morally curved alternatives. The ship is flashing back and forth at the time, the *Responsibility*, the images careening. The waves burn down the bodies of sound and cup them.

Walk through it. There were buses stretching alongside town, slow then they sped up. Her keeper had become famous.

People say or write things not to anyone but a concept of the peasantry, the low-bar simulacrum of a following – "you could walk through the lines on your hand, they would be crevices and you would walk through them for hours longing for a drink" – salvo to a town wall across the bricks and the round post Girl read or those were the words construed. Those spread words red and blue thick lines. Moving her face. "There isn't a grand narrative, so relax." Hhhh. *Keeping comfortable making a difference. That's what it means. You fuck because we're not a species, I am beginning to understand.*

She stretches her arm, still blue from the paint and recognizable lovely to her wet eyes. On land the microscopic bugs at the base of her eyelashes munch assiduously, not the ones thriving in the salt water, *continuity through which you plummet with control.*

She was on her way back to her *atelier* some shared method also comfortable. The day marching feet totally down to circles, the blue sky pinned, meant to indicate willingness, lost in your race to the pickets wherein – except a few – not one day differs from a next. Not one day differs from the next.

She mixes an accidental quality of blood into the last painting of the day. She calls that one *Mutualize*. Not having meant to squeeze out so much.

[Girl considers the moral situation of her conception]

I am in the turbulence of the work, I take the brush and lick it and push it in the paint. I paint the box, I paint the frame then paint the corner in. The corner is wet with oil, turbulent smears. My vision is smeared with my eyes. The corner pushes back in my brush. I dip the paint again and squeeze, the other corner fills slowly and starts to move toward the corner I have already painted. The two corners are moving toward each other, they flex and bow and bend, an option that might open or close, the tears caused by an inadmissible option chain reaction smashing from one to another.

TWENTY-ONE

When she returns they preened and strained. Nearby at the table most conversational distance is sifting mystery, coffee apotheosis, shivering to understand fragments. The ankle bracelet not too bad yes thanks it companys me. After all the self-locking it's a self-defense wait there's a logic.

It's okay, it's okay, that's *your life.*

Awake and all there a braid of self-similarity having gotten hold of her attention with myriad homonyms, she's falling down hard right in the middle of his paragraph so he stops and backs up, not ready yet. He died before they started, the long drive from the city meaning the transition was amenable to change. She read that in the events that happen simultaneous with meanings that accumulate. Not sure what has turned her into a wet stone skipping heavily with the sponges of support along the way. *Nothing hurts here, the radiator burns us all.* She smiles the next day and – deliberate this time – paints her other arm.

Scissors are also tools. A central place in the above sequence and external precisely. She breathes in a long warm breath, hhhh. The psychological remedy essentially committed, windows open to chance,

[LEARNING'S A KIND OF PRISON – YOU CANNOT SWIM STRAIGHT TOWARD IT NOR AWAY]

the eyes looking at her, brown body basking by a square. She continues to address the emphatic collage sensible of the glass and smile. *Passing Vegas to convey this to Degas.* Haha.
She volunteers the elegiac as compensation for the culture's moral worths. Now pushed, now cut-up, even without a cusp she can analogize over where idolatrous natural signs flip out.

There is an outline warm on the floor. The sun shining where she was. She slips into a cool bath chora see-saw, herself a chronograph betwixt the parts.

THE VIRGIN OF THE REMEDIES
The girls she's met arrange a casual art show, compeers, her work among the pieces. Everyone gets half a wall half a floor half a ceiling or the corridor, plus the middle parts of the amiably mongrel stone building. Girl makes an arrangement passable amidst the fulsome salutation as extruded narcissism:
hi gorgeous, you my, mirror elf quite distinct from
what kind of idea are you
in terms of the idolatrous eye gathering concept.
Her calabash was holding quite a lot, admittedly. People agglomerate via the strictures, they hold hands, teaching dualism to their dearests.
You want your druthers and holding them against your curtains as though any minute now they might never burst into flames or be drowned in the commons. But one of the girls persuades her to accept the offer to buy all her parts of the show. Everything, the very next day, goes.

When I walk through these kinds of caves I always think of Forster, you know?
I don't know. Vanishing species with egalitarian narrowness at the top. The druids and their pithy treasures.
Kiss me.

[GIRL EXPERIENCES VISUAL MEMORIES AS PLEATED MEANING]

Girl is moved to make maybe two hundred faces in plaster with
some of the money from selling her art. Human animal, bird animal,
forest tree sky water dirt path animal – what is a sky face without
anthropomorphic unsettling – cows dogs faces, city animal parkway
sharp focused, tea monkey head. The face, books assure you floating
through them, is the main presentational thing: fish face, owl face,
underwater delicacy swooshing face that is not a face, a no eyed
smooth thing cold and managed. *The page is a face*, look look. Wave face,
darling face, mother face. Ama flick held focus, truant skein. Traducing
negotiable here on in, but she's always needing that liquid exchange that
comes in body parts.

She holds the scarf to her mouth looking at the sassy person, regarding.
Ship face. Dialog is the generative third in the room. What is the face
of a spread-out infusion. Perfume, arm in arm, an ongoing relationship
with pasts.
This very kind indigenous percale becomes you.
Moving like languages through the set, the sassy person looks with eyes
like mobile marbles keeping Girl awake trying to allow his syntax.
I'm so tired to be. There is a runnel starred through you. Kiss me!

BARE LADDERS
The basking shapes so attached to their indemnity, so promised to
continuity without any promise back, the pale splotches of meaning-
making bring their skins to seed, to ends of rivers and dives, to
compensations of ideal vomit, to wonderful swirls of poverty colors,
then they graduate to violent admissions, to beating each other with
sticks and spades and gun butts and hoes and clubs and branches, the
violent admixture of sentiment, to hitting and shouting and exploding
and raping, lying and planning and winning, all those precious
accommodations to fortune people make here as they smiled, as the
sassy person smiled, as though the genetics of her plans weren't smeared
all over and inside her own head.

[GIRL SELLS HER ART. SHE MAKES SPECIES FACES]

118

You cannot keep everything in front of your mind every moment without cease without transparent languishing; and repeat. Here, I will help you build mental boxes, let's start. Here's a purple one, into which can go those reflections on glorious despair. The blue one is for calm resignation, the red for indignity and passion. Her skin at night is shadow. *Our color schemes here are not quite stable but still* we flash at them, we open our clothes when the green light comes. He wants to help, cull the self-as-other. His whole body is italicized with determinate meaning.

Bare ladders, on which no one sits. They climbs them or eats them in seasons. *Let me read to you while you paint.* The lavish acid eating in the ears, the floated sentiment of the skin tone. Barley, barley, her body bloats a little one more each day.

He turns the page and reads aloud. The accommodation of the read words to the saturation of movement across the canvas. The genre of the read words she tries to keep out of her eyes.
When you sit like that telling the spare emoluments of your breathing.
When you see pretty clearly the structure of raising an object that is actually an event with trajectories. When you don't need to lie because there is no pain, except the possible intrusion of a non-controllable fate.

All these matters are in your hands that are empty of everything but the obvious. A sofa, a screen, a bus ticket, meals, languages, small plans, reasonable observations, income, nodding, ideas and plans about death. The transfusion of the uncentered face through the medium she seeks. Lovely when it smacks you in the head you were expecting it.

But how could that be? It did not seem possible to say yes. The distractions of insistence on focus, on solidified encumbrance, on threads as the one real wager of social competence. But the agreement was clear from the very beginning, though its clarity is of the shaky kind. Come

[GIRL REASONS ART IS SHORT AND LIFE IS LONG]

along, come along with the one true promise of change. Its invisibility is beautiful, painted in hues. She packs up her favorite brushes and sponges, her gill scraper, her favorite hammer and pallet, her favorite scissors and feathers, her bitumen amperes, her paper and clothes and drawing book. *Hhhh.* Her inner world, her belly, grows.

Breathing

She woke up after the crash in a valley. It hadn't been so bad though the driver giving her a ride had – gone somewhere? She woke up in someone's house. Outside there were spreading lands with agricultural products. These turned out to be, right here by the house, apple trees. What had apples to do with a body with blue arms? You crunch them with your thick teeth and they sink down moist in your belly, moving inside you with the wiggling fish.

She smiles walking far enough away and finds a river near. The little holes for breathing creep out catchments. *A shock is like war in the everyday: you turn yourself around inside and make up a new life with what's available.* The accident did that here and now, and Girl can see she *understands.* Eventually she stays for a while, helping out the little daughter, teaching her to paint.

The daughter taught her

Mollycoddling. Tiny strips of food objects. Painting food objects to eat them without your fleshy mouth. Soon the daughter desires to include words in her drawings, it happened *natural and regular,* she was not showcasing exactly but modifying, aggregating. The words transpire back and forth into squiggles, half-shaded monuments to tiny math. Girl is interested in the additives, like if water had concept that was not performative.

Does water have concept that is not performative?

[Girl flees the illogic of cultural narrative]

120

At dinner that evening. You define your parameters and can say almost anything is inside them.

A kind of ideal parent figure nods at them. This valley is fine because nearly everyone's eating regularly and having adequate manifestation opportunities before they die in relative peace. The soil turns like very heavy pillows, the clouds live on the tops of houses. In the afternoon the adult bodies gather detritus and burn it quietly watching. Floating off the ashes just a little quicker.

Doe

All of Girl's *mistakes* are with her body, truncated wet tongues packed softly a mile out giving way to further attributes: a closed door, empty window, and blank pockets felt as procedural, some dim papers folding to address, limp survey left off, a thinning day too startled to be helpful.

The daughter painted black strips, runways, additives, frames, within relation to color blocks like apple, sediment, sky. Slow parceling of black root lines finely penciled then filled in their long rectangulars.

You could get books and do anything with them, awa. Girl sat in the bath, a tank for questions devoted to inner commas, *nomina mea vestries sunt*, gently sick in the book. Girl licks the side of the stony bath. The books float face down in the warm water.

Stock day

Ordinarily catching the stock phrases he was there with fire in his hair screening making ordinary Girl unlike a strange place deliberately called upon: she is mixed with elements of what one used to be *before consistent character became necessary, theory notwithstanding.* The frontier has entered the brain and devours the remnants of what it meant to improve, so we are without limit in image but needing more at present: who

[Ad hoc governess]

knows what it was like for anyone before, whether anyone else exactly crawled from the sea, certainly not at that point though traces are everywhere? Apart from the normal flash beliefs she's heard about, every piece of youth a moistened cake, *going somewhere exotic only makes a private difference.* When people are alike they only twist against the wall. In a language without such legs, the organs are full of referents, the river pumps ambiguous thrall, lagoon visions in a series of partitions Girl flashes before her eyes.

You know when you are doing something and you don't want to stop: she didn't know when someone would bring her water, so she wasn't free to concentrate with perfect disregard. It's been a problem for some while. How to interrupt one action when another one folds across it. You know how that is, your having to move to something when another action forces itself on scene.
Everyone in animal feels this way, the daughter told her, but that elides the copper props of sameness.

Girl is thirsty. She has a series of indefinite conditions that might as well be hanging above the mantelpiece, between the artistically arranged wooden fragments, some kind of stakes riven with dismay as they waited for the bread to rise, her legs heavy as though inevitable. One side of the conversation was spindly, disfigural, like a phone dialed in to longing, her face a score for modesty and past-ness, names lit more for ladder's sake. Girl stands here now later in brief.

She sees someone with a ventricle attachment and wants to help. Not the body with the body but the outer fold made available. What we learn in the sea of our adoption *one place means other cultural equations.* Her eyeskin watches what difference it makes disappear.

[EARLIER IN OUR NARRATIVE, GIRL TAKES A BATH. THE PRESENT TRIES TO PERSUADE HER]

LISTENING

Provided with a luminous dial, this one can be dimmed and glowed with little bulbs and statuettes. The branches move querulous against the window by the dim river.

She put her art objects up, reaching for the sand shapes, the ladle, the compressed air, the loft a kind of grave artery of scene where she could self-relate. *This is a story like no other, strewn along the fences blown carefully by the attentive wind, west to east, while she against its made directions moves.* It's just stuff, you know, same as difference internally her swelling progress. She's standing here, lying here, representing a long time. Doors open and close.

Some one to bring her water but not a servant. He comes up to her loft and pushes against her, the penis going inside. She feels her skin loosen slowly as she moves her blue arm sideways, the grooves of her thoughts assume wide parallels never more to feed or "remember." The incorruptible paint moves down her arm, never changing its tempo, the tinning of corporeal leaves high up on this side, apart from the subsistence of the trunk. That one that way and the pocket of the *pregnancy* her own.

HOT ART

Plug in all the lights she prepares to demonstrate the work of illumination on surfaces. The rippling needing to continue indefinitely so the fabric in front of the bulbs moves in continual heat. She moves slowly in the heat. Form is energy's inception. A shellac on the painting surface spreads there indefinite shiny opaque. Pant pant.

What Girl wore to the embrace was putty, erasing coverture that made her skin malleable and plasticized, lovely like kneading bread she

[THE HOUSE MAN DOES NOT RESIST HIS IDEA OF THE GUEST]

laughed dangling with an easement her wind-blown surface felt as warm but never wholly protected by a reticule whose thinking was too fervent for dry land. Every surface is umbrella here. She knows hunger is never a proper sign except of *memory* in these parts, the what she does not lack nor have.

In these parts we don't talk of wasting hours theory hands resting behind the back never wounding or causing exactly, more relatable to your juncture than that. Aperture as a formal way of saying *will you have me* in the coherent angle, eyes opening to a famished light, your docking never optimal but offishly compact, not tread enough but translate.
Pester pester.

Dinner gets more complicated the conversion rates keen or silky, the daughter moving into a zone of hindrance a talking beast a face. She rolls her eyes at Girl whose age slips differ. The talk meanwhile is clever as deer tracks leading to the boat, they take us down to sullen water infinitely far from where Girl missed, infinitely regressive steerage ceremony to hold off the noise when you want one, no matter how standing over the body of your own water as though peeling might release – but tender, half-knowing.

WEATHER
Rain kept them in all evening and the noise of unpeeling her eyes from the green material behind her head is soft as water, her mouth a very soft feature aloft clear underneath pooling something another being might feel as words. She listens in silence to the number of stories being told, grange longing, blood warming without that lithesome anti-parallel of sea to keep you cold. He was all about *I gave in* to this openness and one hand drops the conjunction voice seeking to be final threads divergent on the streams against the green and upturned kitchen floor.

[Talk as wet boundary values]

Her tenderizing body parallel with the land, lofted and encumbered though it's always someone else, a visitation. *Nonhomogeneous value conditions render up the question of conducive identity elements.* Water soil water soil. Listening is what the held-in fish-baby body can do.

The complete surprise of being unable to move in the face of an allegory of power. The walls. Wedged in solid air behind her back a vision of honored binaries moving along.

Your prescience meets its volley – *it does matter to some people* once you breach. He opened her legs with a soft finger. A tall white space coveting spleen, a rigged jeopardy able to take the place of a thought Girl is trying to clear up. It isn't the tropics managing crops without water. It isn't the agricultural fields drinking and drinking what little there was. An animal fled softly through the same terrain and yet it was so visible, sibilant visibility, mouth awhisper with sheaves from ear to ear rustling fled cease. *These concept right and wrong, whose are they?*

That, said the thoughtful guard, is a valley throw, a fair sequitur, an honored binary forced to its knees. The guard in the sense of talking person. She, the bucket, the fickle window, all no closer.

CELL
He held her down and pushed and made her voice turn into nothing tangent; of a sudden she could sing she sang she on the floor sange troubadour beloved broke apart.

He was a cleverer, he adapted, he wrote her words to go with his thrust in her sticky substance salty pushing
'til a day I picked triumvirate and blew myself away, the eyes looked once at my own death impossible to feign the happiness they both surmised

[HOW DO YOU LOCATE DESIRE'S PERMISSION TO WANT?]

125

I see you straight in front of me the world bends round my vision twice reverberates, like sound.

Yes but where were you born?

In the water someplace.
I don't think of *as home*.

Authenticity is always happening someplace else, you grock. Because this conversation is "interesting," she wrapped herself in videotape by way of a slow answer. Empathy or metaphor, story stairs. She is becoming visible with stickers, *a self-guided tour through the cosmic mirror, honey.*

Yeah I totally invest that tally, really glue to it, screen your obviously devoted arm-like brain wrapped around itself choke-style.

I mean we could keep talking until *the invention of time* makes us watch the fly careening around our meanings and stop.

He parted the videotape. The daughter watched her.

TRUST SHACK
In the middle of the field in the middle of the veldt in the middle of his mind some treated timber, a passel of nails, an excellent hammer, gravel, concrete blocks, plans for a pent roof, plywood sheets, roof purlins, cladding board, fair barton. He planned all that and she was watching. A bed a chair a table. Desire finds infinite forms. Getting the hang of the local.

She heats up her body and the fire. Like the self turns into spread-along patterns with rivulets succeeding. Some things to separate out.

[THE HOUSE MAN RENDERED AS A TOURIST LOVER]

As convincing as a change of form. You were there and then and came
out of the water into holding fire.

Because it's love you totally devour, the shell inside a wishing instrument
the underteeth explode, come come, ladle to me your perpetual returns,
the visible world seems formed in love, in having the returns to her loft
you are made in.

The pile of ash didn't move, and there was paper. *Hhhh*. Girl picks a small
bucket and takes in the ash, gathers it up. The paper ready on the wood
she dips her finger in the ash and draws. Lick and draw, lick and draw –
a stroke, a blurred series.

The ash works. Hhhhhh. The paper fills with streaks, the head takes
shape, the gesture of the look.

She ashes out looks on paper, mouths open and closed. Another series of
faces where everyone gets excited dying
*like it's something unique and they don't know anything about it. Everyone takes it
so personal.*

As though it is a surprise, like a gift you are not sure you are going to
get. Like a *gift*. And if someone does it to someone else it's strange. Or an
event, like the death truce gone temporarily unavailable. *There are rules
about these things but everyone has access with the right conditions, that's the
principle ah I get it.*

[AFTER BURNING, GIRL MAKES ASHES ART]

TEN
[Video Silence]

Eye witness
In a further town Girl is walking beside a woman who is talented, her
soft belly crated in a dress, a boxed-out sound impure and oblivious in
her voice as she shares her news. *Hbhh*. They walk along having fallen
in while the company flicked its fingers over the market offerings,
cigarettes in violet habit resumed on the periphery. Girl takes her
impoverished breaths nearby and steers her new friend sideways without
meaning to, the path open there.

The square is full of articles of cloth, of piles of fruit and amber bags,
of a person or two delivering little speeches, massed contentment
winnowing and polishing itself over little silver stakes and edible
promises.
Girl hears voices wander through the wettest part of the air, soothing
and slip-shod compared to the extraneous sociality she's run amidst.
Hbhh. Water is running down one side of the square, a diffident rivulet.

*How shall we impart our song? Do our mistakes lend scissors to our principles
unformed until enacted thrall? I am a cut principle, I hover in the errors of sway
toward a vision of erotic flaw, a sway toward the lapsing of the pregnant body into
having swallowed the world as though it were an eyeball in a really nice person's
head: you push your tongue in to the corner of the eye, keep pushing, get hold of the
wet round thing and suck it out, pulling on the stretching tendons and pup, the eye*

[Girl moves along, locating herself in a new town]

129

comes into your mouth, your throat, and you release it into the darkness. The baby rolls around inside my stomach, dark eyes swallowing.

The surface scars of her tattoos inspire Girl to make pictures with needle melting wire on the canvas, "direct painting" cataleptic thought patterns right around the edges, the flame up close to the canvas making marks, *color oils screened into the tiny metal flecks hot the canvas burns a little put it out, leave the holes, patch the fretwork* mingled oil and flame. Those were the kinds of markets that were possible, those massing people like peristaltic reception standing a propos of this town's need for self-expressed vending.

Her art case was next to her legs. Girl's scarf whirled like a purled indemnity over the scene.

TRAINING

Girl knew she would have a very long time to think about all this, to come. Though lately her pains had been growing and she wasn't as sure *as at first*. The bodies of her friends kept appearing on tables. It was a cloudy day and ascription wasn't as easy *as at first*.

She walks claiming toward the building as safer smiles abound.

Picking wasn't for everyone sent on a momentary journey, kept opened and kept perdurable, ice cubes melting on the sweet of her brow spicy as rain, lapped scores aplenty. Here were whirls, telos meters upright in front of the choir, open mandibles hawing and humming through restraints, hardly any solitude or broken locks anywhere. The little holes for breathing closely span. A man was manly and the fish screamed visual. Putting objects or events in their place, *what is the place they go*. What is the wetness in her mouth syllables, the score in her belly beseeches blindly so far numbly, i.e. *without audible request unless*

[HER PREGNANCY IS COMPACT AND CLOISTERED IN HER BLUE BODY]

130

you put your ears right up against the slightly scoring braces of her sweetly smelling skin.

Open door

Meditation, what is that. Girl granted. She sits still looking at an intense wall, the grains of whose painting revealed a saturated depth her eyes unaccustomed sea walls could not stop. The partitions of granules into tiny crusted particle waves upon whom the eye could not linger. She decides Ramsey is like the sun fish she has known, turned on its side up at the surface for cleaning by the birds, a plucked assortment of pores and veins, a huge thing in the water. Letting that thought go, letting it go. One could pull the parasites out slowly so they wouldn't break, best for the sun fish she has known. Let that one go, let it go. Bring another image of Ramsey lolling at the break, the sun visiting his outline like a fish, the birds gently eating to help everyone, let go. Ramsey was a kind guarder of his own life works that were unmanifest as a whole, let go. The mind must falter toward release, breathe in the dry, let out your water in the air, breathe. Alchemy wished to make gold out of base metals, a change for the water of life, aqua vitae, she stroked on the walk over here a stone, a lapis matter morphing lovely blue philosophorum like the back wall of her eyes when water was all round, letting go. Let go. Matter, matter, the wall gentle the air half-infused with water for her demi-lungs, hhhhhhh. That one time fabric, the wet opportunity, let go, *hhhhhhh*. The wall was illuminating the inside of her skull, redder and philosophical let go. The soft hand inside her own the tree in which she'd lived the inner part of the branches so bent down. Filius the lovely woman who made silver jewelry under the moon, let go. That non-specific knowledge inside, out. She put salt on everything she ate but creamy things that were like the cloudy bodies gathering sea letting go, let go. *Hhhhhhh, mhmhmhmh,* hhhhhhhh, the sun shone down on one part of the dark water you understood that was subject to separation, one's

[Thinking without resolution, Girl grows up]

swimming techniques bringing one around the curve, the moon. The burning after a bite. Let go. Her whole mind is the Dead Sea floating, for which the image of the ruined lake is like a mirror held against the flesh let go, lovely year ears trembling hhhhhh, *mhmhmhm*, hhhhhhh, *the perfect and the broken are the same* let go. The wall looks on in tender solitude. The moisture is streaming out of her body.

SHE'D PAINT THE WORDS
An array of jacket pieces flattened over with paint mixed in with bits of gauze (it was a think license, an idea cloth) she could press herself against when it was dry, almost walk into, almost yield. *I mean the ocean meets the land meets the air that squeaks to the sky and thence back down through the whirl with that heaviness, the quickened body pushing held with incrustations beautiful and dark now that you mention it.*

The other surface, *not your body you are running your hand around to feel the skin under the skin*, like making an art is Girl teaching herself a sliding non-translation from one zone of visitation to another: body here, bent fingers, tires screeching on the wrong foot, ties twisted over a hundred bags of sandwiches, thin frames of animals reaching, themselves fixated on fabric toggles in the complicated grass, a blinking of shore lights or the retribution of airplane's blank exterior roar.

She painted shut the books. A solid pile massed together filigreed with painted hair, a full half of the corner weighted pile, a full corner of the borrowed room jammed with painted books. Shown and not shown. Heidegger is dangerous, Ramsey had said, brain butter for Nietzsche in his pieces dislocate. Wrap him in pieces and contemplate them disparate.

She takes scissors and cuts the hair into narrow segments, short like pubic length, gathers it together and mixes it with paint. Body-thick paint, with the skin cells and hair roughness.

[GIRL IMAGINES WORDS ETCHED INSIDE CELL MEMBRANES . . .]

132

A rivulet holds her thoughts now barter signals, water, she's kept warm by latitude imprisonment (like water arrows slicing out impiked in sky), the stars all peeps of brilliantine dislocated on a far-swept old-fashioned machine for mountebanks to ride. The machine pumped behind her in the stables. Several pictures follow.

ARC

The animals went marching over the divided gods, the little beasts slithered through the pantry, the dispersal of focus on the hilly ranges, the innumerable named demi-gods inhabiting differential pieces of the troposphere, the rumbling of ground and unguent baseline hit bottom in the ocean and the toppling of air squirt smash surface light sky, clouds and thundering, the holes in the body and the transactions and the peeling inside out when enough people or other animals gathered and could perfuse their deciduous hungers through the electricity of *no blame*.

TATTOO

You could hear him playing his piano, thunderously communicative in the next house.

She took the needle wrapped in sterile cotton batting and dipped it into the bottle, slight tip, then a slow sewing machine staccato along the lines she'd make, the ink sliding down the needle and entering simultaneously, the lips of the woman staying still while she shrank back away, the soft puff of the lip stunned within itself like biting.

The nearby strings strumming imaginary acceptance tunes, the pale tent soft around them.

The woman is an inverted stilted piece of talking, of screens and causeways occluding superstition, no one was writing it down after all

[. . . SHE MAKES BIOLOGICAL AND LITERATE SCULPTURE]

but everyone in the tent is honed on the downside.

Whispers, wings striping themselves, tiny batting paths. Girl bent over toward her genitals working. Her spine was topside moving.

She makes sandwiches for later, brown bread and fresh butter, taking her time in the hour-shot for the tattoo, some kind of claimant canvas permit serenely collapsed in that dialog.

An uninsured mouth couldn't be opened, she only ever had sketchy leftovers of nerve. She starts humming an interdicted spiritual, fallen off the keys of the nearby piano and taking the place of her silent teeth, fancy and in place of her throat, turning the pages of the map book, projecting a very thin wire to be stretched around the parts when they were finished. *Hhhh*. Girl is still concentrating with her softly mottled arms, the spiritual key outside.

POURING

She met a metal worker, convenient at that time, her sweet hair tumbling around her mask on the hot day. Filius or filial or serial, no more friable or germane obstacles, the cope and drag are excited. The structures are all set up and the sweating of those who were in love with another ceremony, this one body and danger and solid. *They speak in dislocates nowhere near what their chemicals exude!* It would be an artistic burial after all, just in pieces as lovely ash. You could burn it into the metal itself, pattern in swirls. The air shot via particles, like the foment marbles in the deep blue mother.

VOODOO RHYMES

This particular village exertion was worth waiting for, the folks limpet-eyed, the clothing even sterling. Curling around each other in the green

[HER SEVERAL MOUTHS ARE HURTING]

bastion of recurrence, pattern culture and ambient rift, *howdy do and how 'bout you, never really meaning to get too far away.*

You hurt me and I come back, laughed the woman in the evening. Their faces were divided in half and Girl feels the stir of solidarity with their plans. Tea in slow cups, some degree different from the burning hot stuff. Slurp slurp.

She knows she is getting close to water, water pushing around inside her free variation. Following upon the pattern of pigeons, in the evening against the sofa she perched her body and said it was good to mount up from the ocean with your body turning to land, a good kind of mounting of your flesh, taking yourself the fastness spent, like the particles of the water joined around you moving roared reluctant though
I never got so close to anything wild.
No because I want to tell you in time I found the creature red that held its mercy front to back and kept it wholly-half.
What is the performance of getting to know someone?
My moral center's keenly felt, extremity and turpitude free-styling.
This raspy skin a catch to eat, a fur to lick and soothe.

Palate
Increasingly she listened, increasingly the metal worker and her friends made emotional logic clear among themselves; they seemed to mark a tempered spot, a clean collection felt along the hinge of her mouth, the plate, their bodies.

Instead of talent, mark the hour when movement is itself alone they ran with bird cries on their backs then swam right up and felt the water pushing slow to front, bowing to order she candled me, *I thought once more of the soft wet moving cloth shucked, pillaged on the simple space pilaster.*

[Over time, Girl explains herself to the metal worker]

No one in the town had a notion of expecting anything from anyone so they were not prepared to create a story in which she featured, though no one even thought that through nor nobody really minded did they. *You know what that's like, this condition directly related to a life of forgetting.* Forgetting folds forged with palettes of where you are and food-getting bearing up and making ways to divest your memory to a geophysical mnemonic. Falling through. Where Girl knows only insofar as each event's before her.

CANDLE-EYED
To a young person she met Girl is describing a piece of language, like placing your hand flat once definitely upon a large rectangular table full of warm water which absorbs the movement induced by your hand and spreads out within its confinement, a warm multiple pulse shivering the shape.

Where's morality in this he asked. *Hhhh.* Not that she had developed any aversion to explanation, but it was as though she had already explained the problem meaningfully, in line with the same explicable dimensions they rolled around in their mouths every day like topiaries. The appropriate image is never worn to the appropriate room, so far as Girl could see. People's clothes and the images they foster saturate.
Irruption you know that and then
me knowing if and could, the two of you I don't think so!
If the barroom is applicable to that stubbed word
you know best, it becomes fruitless to contest, the game is done.

Which was about as much as conversation could manage, you know how it's so burdened with the function of the talking bodies. *Close your eyes and listen to someone then, let their words grow inside you, accumulate like rain.* Girl has learned a wary approach to usefulness in any event, time being what

[GIRL REFUSES THE ABSTRACT-TANGIBLE DIVIDE]

136

it was since the woman she knew had joined the orchestra to sing with her pipes, to get away with the piano next door.

There's frigging time and there's loving it, Girl, and which are you.

At night, Girl's blood joins the air and feels plucked, matted, folded over. In the morning before she realizes anything it is a clear stream. Hhhh. The little holes for breathing feel like electric eyes, small needles without pain. The partitions of the body pocketed without pain, *loving you*. The waves of air separate the water into pools with open eyes.

Trial
She ducked out leaning on the air, honorably misanthropic she had become tired, constantly thirsty, arraigned busy wavering.
In the afternoon by the stream she throws in many pieces of bread. A will-of-the-wisp malingers on the way down toward the gap-eyed lake, more rain, more still, youth's fair flight under the giant-making sky fitted for accurate mind to stray to an irradiated opening called *hope* or illumination.

Across her teacher's bland narcissus walk Girl had spoken crossed-out, wandering by ribbon-waving trees who spent the light night folding sheeting crisp branches lifted away. It was helpful she had never had any real papers, walking out from whatever official versions of events were needed to construct a parity of cultural returns. Aquarium. One in one out one bad one punished.
It was spoken in the side room, a smile and weary, they wanted you to say something meaningful and you studied the words. Agriculture, aquafarming, admonishment. He was a lovely boy in his dell.

From that hour she nestled alone, willing to *shack up* but not to *sleep with* whom she met who might wish to burrow but never insist on sharing

[At night her pores open. Her colors move]

the venues of actual sleep. She is so young they kept saying. She is *tabula dilation,* but it isn't enough to call it art. She is irrelevant to the furnitures of culture on which she sits and stands and moves her pulsing torso embabied.

GRATITUDE
Thank you for the trail of messages hitchhiking the road
less traveled on the beginning of the first
day blood on your acetylene dress
idyllic spent shells of someone who lived next door and always seemed like such a
nice man

"She came in often and always had a smile"
and your heart will weaken transplant target bear mauled by the camper
then left alone under the tree above the swamp near the house with
windows whose blind eyes are the lids of the content soul, wind rhythm
and water lapsing against the corpses of the birds, insects, tiny reticules,
other particles mingled with strewn soil
my feet will never be clean again.

So sorry to you young seeker, you will answer yourself and then be
galled. She never washes her mouth with soap but her words were
always so clean, her hands always tickle the rocks she throws into the
stream flowers decorating her parcels. She always thanks the screen
folks when they leave, but Girl never understood any gratitude lying
around before and she certainly isn't starting now.

[ON LAND, GIRL IS VERY YOUNG]

ELEVEN
[LATTER DAY]

The gene-based happiness set-point theory was all over the news, she hears it echoed on the radio those vibes paralleling the micro-particles of breathing; the birds were also singing next to those waves whoo-ee whoo-ee and she hears them singing, *shhh, shhheeeh,* her ears not false though one might think their adaptations were not so friendly to the crazed air-suffused environment *which is more than I can say*; she finds turning the radio dial that her ears turn internally to the switched micro-stream inundated with properties.

So what did she hear, what sonics.

She hears about sound proof booths and thinks it would be like *pornography* for her to visit one, she could be alone and not hearing the micro-streams operate, as though brought to a point of contact or sail the bandwidths spread out merciless. The little holes for breathing contract and expand in contact with their multiplicity, her skin contracts and she becomes who you are talking to. *The concern of recent events,* the relentless discussion of recent events, causes the skin inside her ears to become raw as the internal pores suction out the multiple streams that stick to the waxy surface like musical burn points. The number of days in her

[GIRL LISTENS TO THE RADIO. THE PLANET IS A RADIO]

139

pilgrimage are in inverse proportion to the next baited piece of timely conversation swinging on wires, caught in affect like prayer belts – the sound might flow out and into the receiving sunfish, the sword dial, the atavistic ray turned into a machine for the cocooning of the animal arrayed in a physical limit. Irresistible to love the growing other inside, like a recognition of your borrowed state. Hhhh.

What does her throat feel like.

As if Girl has swallowed a box of magnets and gone polar the water-like air comes close around her, almost like a cloak, almost allusive and dark-securing, like that sound booth she imagines when the other might finally stop, wishing to secure some peculiar bandwidth she might hear, the little holes for breathing burned for ears.

Where is that voice coming from? Her tendency to hear water everywhere, in the ground under her legs, in the pocketed air, meant that Girl can't always locate these sound-aerated movements, where they are when, from what direction? *I mean pornography in that she would forfeit regular desire machines of talk and listen, listen to the events around you allow them to take you, I mean it's an irruption an interruption and a seizure – so this booth, a specific catalog of wishing outside the bonds of naturalized doing, that's the porn.*

Her art is trembling sideways, smiling dog-like in her conception taking an instant liking and disseminating it, spread over the walk over the surface she keeps moving to see more accurately and hear (that's why you do it, you keep moving because moving is being-meaning, there's no replacement for it).
She was suckling a seal in her dream last night, dark-bodied, young, saving it, its strong body in position, shallow water having come from a

[Her maturation diffracts into multiple voices]

female who wondered aloud at the mutability of her face, a smile is not a smile but manipulative of what's to come and glow romantic: "go," your youthful fires gleaming forth as from a distance, corridored alongside the building where that pouring had been, long after the garden party, as one dream here replaces the next.

Her body folds inward on its little holes for breathing, the skin moist strewing, the red sheets tangible.

You could keep going, the glow is not replacement. The house she is next to now was built that way, each room a new color and light announcement through the windows she is being led in, a friendly conversation escape via faces, voices, one's own folds in upon itself until it's crumpled,
I understand you, you miss that,
coming around like heat evaporating into shallows, walking into shade only to be met, artery, one always wanting to understand, to make the pass direct the perfusion monumentally construed as a local act of comprehending you, this action is to make another and increase the mass so as to make a "showing," so as to enfold one's collected rivets on their frames spread out across a giant ball of air. Housing sounds and paint walls. Time's *passing.*

Then it was more than one person talking after all, it was a small collected multitude.
We are like that we talk *we understand each other* she hears it named a *vulva,* that is nice, get ready for something a collect call coming across the circuits hurt her ears enormously, that cut the thread, she stays quiet in her room all evening wetting.
The tank of earth beneath her hummed and ground's thick flesh was sucking underneath.

[HER PASTS AND PRESENTS PERFORM CONNECT]

And she squiggled with pleasure in contained moments. Syllabic
consonantals striven with glee. Their particular cabal was propitious
though she had a resigned misgiving about the nature of the exchange,
even at sea there was always compromise, you were always having
to move even when it didn't feel like propulsion was the order of the
universe necessarily, it wasn't a question.

Yeah that's a temporal manifestation of the fact that lately she's been
learning to blink in a different way or as a matter of belief it's the small
faces upturned for modeling and quite still that move her. Gentle mottled
hands full. Growth pains.
She holds the paper with a longitude but having heard she's now a
latitude, the center tracking center's inlay, an astounding diameter.
The dump is perfect, trashed and serene.

The gaps were the thing that *most shows*. This part of town has many
languages, some with and some without. If she cannot paint with facility,
we might think, so what?, closing the gaps, lessening with increased
felicity script buried in paints. *She writes words, i.e., and paints over them so
she knows they're there.*

Girl rebuffs the syncopated titles and family trees being offered in
this medium, no titles, text panels hand-drawn and purely informatic
– so logos, so going back and forth without severance. Whereas *post-
Mallarmé, post-Muybridge, post-alarmist* she hassles herself into compliance.

Dark matter sustains the paint she does leave there, activated for a set
of reasons equated with the value of new mediagraphy. Be met, and
pay attention to the colors that rhyme. Her singing chords so high they
strangulate, unhearable.
When you start to understand you split from yourself and become voices.

[GIRL TRIES TO BE ART]

Afterward, her legs run against the grass the length of time she painted, a voice heard elongate spinning across the trick of having to serve, a block stands there in the domination of a waiting-to-go-in that seems to expect her for fulfillment. When "go" is the open-minded attitude of the wandering eye, her chic opportunities are soft under the influence of such means.

You've been at this for a while. What is that, what do you mean. *My apologies.* No no, it's ok. What increments of manning are you showing me.

SHOWING
You could take some cash and exchange it for some small materials. She could make a chain link fence paint piece isn't it, the sequential guarded as clover, the sucking parts stitched in perhaps to incubate sticky-out particles underwoven with a slow trickle of friendly spleen given what can happen between here and fifty feet away
if we can get that perspective
and a really big building where thousands of tiny speakers might be crying. The canvas thicker and thicker as she stands near. She puts more on this one for several days, the secrets of underlain paint excruciating. Girl absorbs the borrowing, penitent beforehand nevertheless crawling under the wire fence pieces
the light shunts down remarkably!

Walking continuously by ditches not looking or thinking about the arch *betrayal* that is after all irrelevant in the long run, something to get that she could implant in the fence-work, an implant to *see sound* exceeding tiny valley crones tucked in the hemistitches; only to make this happen she needs to kneel in the gravel to produce the right impression, a window that blocks out the light. Her tummy to block the light.

[GIRL MELDS PAINTED CANVASES TOGETHER SO HER ART IS PRESSED INSIDE
IMPOSSIBLE TO SEE]

143

At purchase time she thought about the globules rising sense rippling as a wall, not ground for worry *which it is not,* she is intent staging the small particles luminous and returns in the evening to a cellar circle.

In the circle were people gathering in patchwork belief, very contented persons needing to find an excision of the neediest part *we have a prejudice greeting everyone at the door*
the point arises with a laugh and forsakes. *Hhhh.*

You name yourself a task and you become that task-name. Her tummy flips inside. She is going to have to pick the lock to get out. She could imaginatively break the contents afterward, she wouldn't really need to deprive those who had acquisitively named the piece *their own*, declaring many feet on the floor this focal point seeming to indicate some good taste filled.

She is spread dissidently backward, that sassy person rolled up the stairs her sentence left behind toward Girl who optioned an increasingly dismayed sense of departure like the point at which the fencework met her wooden stool, the prop choice drying out between sessions with other people meshing *rockabye, coal-struck, baby-eyes* while Girl still slightly loving them with her mouth fills out her plan, eating one tenderly.

TELLING
Doesn't it become you, dear. Girl thinks when talking to people of how their faces will look in a hundred years, floating dry and wet, heavy and light, all bone, nothing in the eye sockets, so much more interesting to believe the conditions that makes those people say what they said at that moment.
Oh like Persian and Mara – delicious pets –

[ORIGINS DON'T CLARIFY. HER MOTHER AND HER FATHER ARE DIFFERENT HOLES]

they keep starting anywhere and giving up, turning the conversation this way and that, theoretical logic collapsing over and over again picked up, the temperate and judgmental caves in their heads giving out and sucking in, glowing and refusing, getting somewhere in a mind sense, a moving thing a loop – *I know this drill* the body going ever forward but not necessarily getting someplace so much as going, we do this.
A condition in which everyone could have a go: *I know an I as compared to a you I have evoked, let me tell you listen.*
Girl says enough to keep it rolling, surrounded by wet mirrors. She sits that afternoon looking patiently through one frame at a time, the completely slowed image.

How could knowing become instinctive in such acts? Rustling, *hish hish*, score and woody bone beneath. They move like the cloaking of innumerable leaves and you can actually see it.

She is pleased her body had been given forward, I mean this shifting gills to pores, a causal permission that prepared Girl to see the deciduous trees totally toss off their leaves, hooray, the shrunken anatomy hold itself in a differentiated atmosphere.

The hills were long jaw bones talking from the moving car. Such a child sitting beside her, that other daughter whom she missed, she realized, repeating and repeating the points from the film she had seen repeating the words to a song that revealed her access to that disappearing light in the middle of the old television screens when you shut off the telly and the pinpoint rapidly inverted and swallowed itself at the center of the screen – the little girl was like that. A series of vanishing historical images presented simply because Girl's mental images appear.

Can I touch it what does it feel like?

[DAUGHTERS SHIFT THROUGH DIMENSIONAL SIDES OF EARTH]

Girl suggests she came from a world in which the trees were born small and wet and either folded or enlarged continuously, sort of like young ground trees come to supplant the elders with a gentle wet replacement that yet did not imagine itself that way instead entirely involved with *being*. And no one she had known before was all hot about how things were supposed to last.

The belly fronds itself, makes her arithmetic to appearances, *yes go ahead, you can touch*.

People make room for you in the logic of territories but not really. No one is necessarily *you* come to pass by turns getting closer though they look for the *I* in *you* like rivuleting ocean bats turning slowly round, and slowly around, enlarged by their experiences. Events penetrate and like the glue on the quay growing up around your anticipation you hold it there, you frieze it.

She had the portion of the fence work, she could carry that with her, symbolic of the array of persons who had claimed or helped it. And photos of her paints and storyboards. So many slightly altered starting points and how do people imagine "common" sense or an adequately unhinged personality profile flying across the satellites?
Space is very like the sea, flotation, a portfolio, motile abjects and size invasions, regimens to flash. At any omen what you see becomes the clasp you see by frame by frame.

If you slow the images down gradually, gently corral their borders, they become words drifting in the water.

STORY
I guess that got communicated: Girl's interview is successful, and her new

ʟ UNDERSTANDS HER EARLIER CONVERSATION WITH THE METAL WORKER] job is to illustrate a book of stories by a woman. The woman lived in her barn at night so she could hear the horses shuffled breathing. She gave over story ideas without the writing which helped Girl with stories stuck in her head as she drew graphite sketch after sketch, penned in the nib digs, further into thicker and thicker paper. She makes the sketches grimmer and grimmer but further and further away until the woman whose imagination formed this trick found the accompaniment acceptable, the veer of the lines. They *understand* each other.

STORY ONE

A boy escaped to the woods only to be put to the test by three supernatural beings, one of whom put the boy's head in a vice, or rather his whole body, with a series of reactive tightening repercussive gadgets strapped and pulled together, and then the supernatural man struck with a mallet upon a target, which made the pulleys and levers tighten and tighten. Ten times he struck the target, and at the end the devices leveraged sufficiently to smash blood from the boy's head and ears.

The boy pulled the gear off his body, knowing the test was over, and blood washed out on to the forest floor.

That was all right in images. He got in a line of persons imagined and real being tested for matching with a supernatural partner. All mismatch and danger: a boy with a non-human animal, a girl with a skeleton, shadow figures diminishing through the forest spaces. The emotional wires were cut across the supernatural partnerships, and the blood and forest had no feeling.

The boy was overjoyed in the shadows. His containment came in sentences.

[GIRL GETS ILLUSTRATING WORK]

STORY TWO
A community of people displaced by natural disaster breathed and ran. They wailed and were rendered sterilized until some other arrangement was put in place. They turned to new homes, places of theft and rugs on the floor and individual purchases. A series of rooms that fit into each other, but they didn't like living so close to each other's wretched mirrors.

The story turned to one particular evening. A film was on the television in the new location; it was the test. There was a complete separation of house persons: family and yet not, hallucinatory couplings. They had painted each successive room a mildly changing color paint, the doors transitional, individual apartments. A young girl smiled with happily doomed fatigue and soaked the cloths in water. She lit the fire. Nothing.

Nothing had changed in the disaster.

ILLUSTRATIVE
In a similar vocabulary Girl is apt for her employer.
How you get somewhere or are we trying to get closer to a set of languages in which people see themselves but not too close.
Girl makes her face blue with white vertical streaks along the sides. Her fit bore in nonesuch attachments. Those who had been de-coupled from the culture around them found her defenestrating, i.e. when they all sat together pauses rattled through.

The season turns a little. *Time passes.* The employer lends her a horse from the barn, riding underneath her, rasping the saddle, hands on the bridle. The horse shivered beneath her with a patch of draft straw the bridle semi-taut the saddle blanketed and firm. Girl's legs split wide on the saddle her big belly over the leather the smell of animal the slow ride animal knew how.

[IMAGINE HER ILLUSTRATIONS!]

She holds the belly on the slow ride animal thoughts, the little holes for breathing open slightly, the horse huffing out through her nostrils warm wet out Girl holding with her legs. This animal knew. *Hbbh.* Three beings longitudinal, enormous entire horse body. Not like the trial or bestial car, no hinges holding. The tendrils of her bloodstream fondle those inside the horse imagination. The horse shivers in its traces, buckling.

ESSAY ON SECRECY
Perhaps especially apt in an era when people salutarily understand they are not highly individuated but rather made up of patched-together recurrent typos. Such a stance would explain the ready yielding up of information and images formerly considered, in some cultural contexts, private.

Unlike Girl's oceanic origin, in which the particular is real because the water is too silty for events to be seen anywhere else other than where they are happening, despite the allusive archiving done by supernatural visitors, those swimming bodies tanks of steel, the visiting human. They get that, the particular and context slipped between. Except the memory of rush and its correlate water highways, company. What is visible from five hundred units away? From another medium? The translation for Girl from there to here is the desire to multiply one's interior to make the area compensate for the total visibility allowed. Measure, measure, horse and rider, water wheel.

Under a tree alone Girl touches her hand along her arm, the little holes for breathing gently flinch. Secrecy to exteriorize cavities untouchable by everyone, as though your personal space expands in secret, sexually and thoughtfully providing dance floor under space without responsibility, fluctuating singular as partial knower and still the knowing as complete, like wearing perfect skin for the first time.

[WHAT NON-HUMAN ANIMALS KNOW]

"Natural literacy" she said out loud though alone, being the reach across to another, the thing flooded with apprehension not to be misunderstood any longer, on one side the perfection of mortality and on the other a mere picture. For Girl to understand meaning must be a vacuum in order to assume the proper proportion with sense. That's knowing, separate from *to do* and live.

She sort of understands this in her growing torso source as electric thickening body. Under the consequence lies the next spectator, who doesn't know what will hurt in a field for feeling fracture, disassembly, distance takes the air out of Girl's heart and lets it petrify the sky, its endless option an embarking wave pushing out the shelf where she is never trying to persuade anyone. Much like a prehensile "man alone" imaginary, Daphne who can correlate at will, getting ready to graph invisible tectonics at the top of the sky.

GROOM
This arid land is something negating her secrecy. She plucks pieces out of the wire and rock, a standing body makes its appearance through a day of lethargy, of fanning her hair out over the rocks.

Girl rents a van and sits in it for a week, her heart rinsed with washing fluid and dripping on the strainer, it pulses her eyes shut against sleeping to be reverse, to make the tallest lack of promise mobile on a reverent vision, *hhhh*, these people in love with the grapes nearby, not too far away after all, words straining toward watery windows her cup fell circumstantially on the counter of the van. A tolerance that is *don't make me notice you.*

Travel is an accurate sensation, it promotes wires of annihilation crossing underneath her eyes with a permanent lack of foresight except for the blanket expectation churning out the gravity ahead to give her

[THE BODY IS VEHICULAR]

flower feet something to walk on, her wet bones secret by the polished van door, thirsty, the map inadequate but for another mode of plan, wingspread flourishing shadows grazing on the stipple grass the pointillist trees by the sparse river, shots broke her ears but were just desert boys completely ruptured, ringing a clotted sound along the thickening of the track, the whisking trees in majestic refusal her arms at just the right density it's permanent – the suspension altruistic, no the boys nearby on polished air strokes – the entire surface is made of fingers pressing to escape the impress, muffled by the hair pulled back the air sucked from its water unraveled from the outside, the van subject to a wax drip solvent clearing the place the blue takes on percussive strikes repeated, the van out of gas – no where consequential burrs felt in, pedestrian hazards fleet and tremor of the held plastic jug so that round is what to look at means, a preference for ridges stripped layers rasping on the heat context, some never-before-visited faces, a preference for what might equal never asking, though her body's very hungry, an evacuated hurt among the separated trees.

There are not enough hours in the day for tending her hair, not enough days for keeping her skin full, her little bracelet made of bones rattles but not as well as her language does; it seems one can inveigle into the dreams of someone with an open heart door and just *tend* there if you language match.

This group shares its symbolic references rapidly with Girl, the externalization of cultural norms in rapid patterns, easily co-conceivable by her hands and tongue, *communal.* Foreshore ideation is still in her future, but she has been rescued by these *fedayees* we'll call them, some old compatriot circumstance that binds or blinds them, eye-sucking strategies for self-nourishment. They co-inhabit symbolic identity rather than their names, whether or not *understanding.*

[AFTER THROWING OFF EVERYTHING, GIRL IS AGAIN TAKEN IN]

Girl has a contributory value, she knows that, and she is looking for
nothing more from this place, though she realizes final value made
her extend her stay along. The land animals teach her nothing of
ultimate use *qua* whatever that might be, "use" being instead causal,
predicate, "interesting" – nothing, that is, she could take "back" with re-
submergence. Could she.
What was the imagined agreement her sharkish heart could wait for?
The enormously long valley canyon pitches.

DIDACTIC CONSTITUTIONAL
Legged in symbolic irons, her new clothes return her very near the
shore. During her communal time with the fedayees, she wrote to Her
wondering if she might be headed, anytime say, to the town Girl was
getting into her sights.

She got a map at the library and studies it for soft spots. The last high-
quality vestiges of her time with art had been left behind, but Girl knows
there are works available kept with friends or patrons from her artistic
immersion. What is the price for leaving behind and asking for the
context to come back to you, available to that, human? *Move move.*

She eats her berries with slow deliberation, her eyes fretting with lashes,
her head and belly pulsing, her legs long arrows point to earth invade.
She went this whole day without speaking. The carmine inner torso
spreading its biology or food, her blueberries she spread on her arms,
and licking the blue.

Perhaps, Girl reflected, not everyone's self-apprehension modifies by
encounters with food. It's more the enlarged things people amass as
examples of such alteration. Travels, for example this narrated
stretch of time, any thing that does not involve constant repetition-into-

[IF PEOPLE UNDERSTOOD THEMSELVES AS FOOD]

unnoticeability. But when your eating involves the immediate disestablishment of a formerly intact substance – the total annihilation of the sandwich, kelp torn from the waving level, little fish ceasing to dart, big fish squeezed after capture, objects wiggling in your torso gulps of sweeping tiny plankton spinach waves – then perhaps you are aware of the still-beating heart grabbed by the hand of a vanquisher in those stories and how eating it gives you that spirit. So it is with sandwiches, cereal, apples, biscuits. They give you their spirit.

Hungry, Girl is puzzled by the non-occult status of eating hereabouts. Like, there was *totally nothing to say* about the food apart from some notation of its hitting the taste bud areas in especially effective or dull ways. It was more like oil or curtains or clothes or vehicles. Not so much like holding someone's hand for the very first time or licking asphalt at the parking lot by the beach or going out at night to roll against the prickly bush without clothes so as to feel the difference between that and sand and grass and fabric and water. Not so much. The information economy is retrograde, deficient in the imbibing consciousness Girl generously composes.

Check the bracelet, turn it deeper, put the new battery in. Where are they reading you from? Can they read you anymore? Why are you still wearing that? Is it something you've had for a long time?

A BED OF WIRES
She feels her flesh baited for fish pain through the icy looks this new person left upon her face. In conversation it is evident Girl had learned a few things, not so much about art perhaps, since she was mostly applying the tenets of what was clearly another world within the graphic and dimensional predictive forces of these *media*.

[BETTER TO BE A TINY ANIMAL, TO UNDERSTAND TINY]

No, it was more like what one of the women had said: she'd learned that people mostly had conversations with themselves, that you were the channeling material of their self-relation. It was funny and even sweet, like with their domestic animals it's clear the animation of the "pets" is mostly a torque device to make sure the human keepers are more satisfied in the sense of the pet being a self-soothing channel, a looping mechanism for a sense of intimacy people want to have with their surroundings in order partly to love themselves. And the silent predicates of pet relation. Like ideas couldn't come that close, like *love*. Otherwise wouldn't the animals have more choice, more self-extrusion in living?

She wishes she could talk with Ramsey, now, about what she's learned. The globulous touches of intimate sex were perambulations into her own veins achieved through direct transmission of chemicals in skin contact. Plus the touching of particular areas. If you didn't touch those areas, it was pleasure. If you did, it was satisfaction — but recurrent, like hunger.

What was the solace New Person could find like a predictive force riveted to guess, with only eye contact, separation modulated through skin angles and body wires?
Was it meant to be a hunt, Girl wonders. Sometimes, and other times a full-body papier-mâché, a shopping trip.

Do you want to turn that instrument?
She lay it flat and ran her fingers up and down the strings, *izzzizzit*, she plucks and opens her mouth. New Person had a guitar, a bold pillow hard enough to correlate.
"Ah, you like music." *No maybe elements extruding on the air.* When you hold it to your belly your whole torso hums and rings.

[EXPERIENCE DOES NOT EQUAL THE EVENT]

Her body hunkers on the cold-invested white of the sheets, she enters through the cavity barnacles and bumps slid through, the topography of her breasts and hulls and arms underneath a cover to be aware the other feels an insufficiency like a real and subsidable shadow, outline falling through replacement doors. She wants her fingers to be as soft as gums. She wants to comfort roughly New Person in that.

[SO EVERYONE'S A REPRESENTATIVE ANIMAL]

TWELVE
[CATCH]

SOUND MACHINE

An outing willing to gainsay, or ready for, her round blue self – dressing
for it was like swathing a wet body in the grimmest finery. A place
where given torsos ramify. Her skin ululates underneath form-fitting
pants and shirt, her belly plumps like palms.

Opera opera. It sits communally and lashes against the velvet stage
rocks, the bodies conjoining personal space, electric tingling in
architecturalized wood frames.

Cool the right glance left to her now, she looks and sees the lit box felt
for time lapse. He walks by, then she wishes the tie bound ship would
stall. This is community anyway, persons with a share.

They sit and the ornamental evening begins although Girl has an
unbreakable urge to move and gets up and down *annoyingly*. Someone
sings of lilt riff – it's jacked from a voice that breaks and makes the time
go lolly in her chest, where the little things are stored for felt boys –
given stage times, dance moves given instrument or – plinked across the
waves she feels the boy go under, *ama* sees the opera, sees the singers
floundering muttering at the wall of rocks between shots – they are
bending over looking at the audience of the very dark home, deliberate
in their gift. Time crashes itself in that.

[NEW PERSON TAKES GIRL TO THE OPERA]

157

Why in the open earth is there not more of such unpeeling?
Culture with the soft water salt streaming over the audience heads
delicious, making their rough flesh sticky in their knife feathers,
reasonable reception of the woman with her face upturned to you for
a spell, for the percept glass made woozy for that glance, *hhhh*, Girl
hanging on the edge. Her mother was like that when the wedge came
in sight. A little time, then the medium and your apartness hinges, you
from me.

That upturned vision *all time playground* spun at night, given to muttering
at the opera that answers back with stakes through the heart, *a shared
experience* overdoing the soft hair of the listeners, waving through the
water leaning in with their permitted candies. Her audience desires to
determine the chords – they lean in with their bodies to the orchestra
of – the ship smashing on the rock and, smile. Hhhhh. The inside of her
belly thrashes and smiles.

The woman seems to listen as her mother listens, hotly listening at the
edge of the strings of the waves, that posture suggesting a recurrent
constancy. The body of the young man turns toward her with a script.
With their lips on the score, the audience leans lower and lower, the top
of the water, the upper balcony, up to the top of the ceiling, right in the
vanishing center, until intermission when they permit each other.

Wrecked for the evening they've come, his paddling replaced by her
strong wrench, not escaping in this version, no, his head devoured
all over the floors of the waves on carpets over the floors of the halls,
into the padded stairs. Girl runs slowly with her vision swayed by the
dominant music that has crept her yielding from the edge of her seat to
the middle of the concert, standing underneath the stairs listening, alone

[HUMANS MOVE LIKE THE CONTOURS OF CLOUDS . . .]

in the red hall without voice or instrument beckoning the wet floors that rise up to meet her.

SELF RELIANCE

It was as if the experience you had existed in no correlative, in the world everyone just went along anyway. How you could be at an event and then no longer there. Its borders removed and all-new flashing and footware underneath.

New Person made another gathering. Girl became certain that people on land partitions led to simple tracks of love and blood and hire. New Person kept on telling her what she reminded him of: fog, moving smoke, creeping fragrant waste of their bodily functions, please hook your desires over the top and here's the kennel, raise them, tell me a story, an explanation, here's mine, panting, hand it back and forth
god is my light and my pilot he makes the stove blow up in my image
they all laughed from similar sets of memories.
You cannot find me in the details of growing things, my bones are formed with spines and prickled hackles, yellow and pink rays formed *for*
the honeysuckle to be itself it must be eaten
he apologized next to the air duct completely unaware. Girl shed off enticings they are scaling from her laughter shakes, the body propped against the wall is shaking, rocks for pillows the hand thrown recklessly down and taken in as though one kind leads to another.

She isn't good at laughing, it's the air problem. We promoted this causality, an economy like unmanaged Jesuitical parsimony, like the exchange rate rising up naturally from the geothermic sutures nearby.

My sister too made plans like this, she traveled across by train though, she made it a little easier on herself (laugh track again),
a cluster effect of knees enjoys Girl speaking in a silent voice, we sing in

[. . . BLOCKING OUT STORIES AND EXCHANGING BLOCKS]

159

the trapped molecular, uphold our brutal glasses, they've made the fire
burn with green sparks, they've made themselves *relatable* with what they
do. "What a lovely time," smiles.
The tones come on, *if your arm is in France can your body be far behind*
(laugh track again)
they have been fine tall strangers ever since he showed up at the
Saturday market, he dropped his hat and she meant to *keep it for you*
perhaps, or donning in English weather.
I found it useful to salute his temperate worthiness.
Your feet exist in obscurity although I love them.

She paints his leftover shoes blue too, *every ounce of cotton in America
gets a little closer to China.* (Laugh track again.) Swath yourself, bathe
yourself, the bath tub handles, you sit motionless in the water, temperate
salt.

There is a swirling sensation when the troposphere arranges itself for
another set of areas, thinking their location was part of the transient
immortality of hope. Girl brings her principles hither without voicing
and he *accepted* them.

ARIAS OF EX
Okay, she could adapt that art to commerce, she took a job making the
small arts prints runs for shops, how you could go in and out of things
and – here was some *food meaning*, she was making the menu for the
coming week and found this café's ominous stricture rites entangled
greenly in elements of dorsal promenade. *How true* whether the patrons
were sitting or the pre-killed entrée plans were sprightly recommenced,
garnished with a classic rhythm, or waiting with a slight perpetual
grimace. The curlicues needed to communicate as though planted in a
ground up top, a cascading thermostat that keeps the whole page steady,

[GIRL STUDIES SENSORY PROMPTS]

curving around flashes that would make the room go dark when you tried to read them making your digestive plans.

Action substitutes were realer and reported with a dull accuracy what had you seen, and how had it made a difference; the light transporting over the ledged drafting desk was the kicking element, just under-reporting how someone had breached the cave barring striders meant to hop over where someone else had been sitting comfortably.

How could an event happen and then cease. She cares *too much*. *Don't be in such a hurry.*
A little like eating the paper the patrons and her own skin. Across town another contractor was planning the music, sermonic witness to make the eating seem a real event, *I take it you have* clasped the simplest *cost available* sealing the envelope with a thin gesture congruent with impermanence, potions made to combination. Colors on the cover, the slip given and assumed as an innocent lingering dimension, the inches treading steadily toward limit.

The whole thing swirled, the novitiate screening, the parallel invitation to join, that the disciple scene was one, her eyes like private showings turn toward this room and that one. They want because wanting makes the objects on which they put their bodies, on which they put on and in their bodies, their mouths. They want because without wanting we all splint on droves, harrier. Which part of the world moves first?

Girl leans back from the drafting desk finished with this one, one hand pressed on the wall, breathing. *Hhhh*. A way to subsist to meet without eating without wailing. The pink cones the blue cones fervent, her insides push sideways. Her feet underneath her pulsing feel like knives.

[Alone with a task, Girl turns invisible]

The birth of feeling

How we like a horizon. Everything on the other side of the distance
flowed into it... her face wide open and crenelated, the feathery flip side
of her hair heavy on her eyes, she wanders in the bristly grass.

The asymmetric rule of ground is giving over slapdash humor rolls... her
sky like lips pushing down so close to shore now. If in the scene it was
quieter than circles, that was for the threat of life pulsing in and around...
leaves in the interim....

He walked with her talking about how to live. *I was once in that hair, I was
once in that eye, I once walked in that shape*... it's a forceful argument, it's an
attitude cruncher but not a fool-proof dispenser, not an end to novice.
He said so in the stupid voice, the one he wears in public though they
were alone, if you sat there for a long time do you think conditions would
become clearer?

What would that wooden fence look like, she wonders, in a hundred
years, if one whittled at it without cease but not meaning to make it go
away... her belly was *all right,* her breasts were moving, heavy waves
moving on the outside of them pushing her body to follow.

When she was attached it was *not let go, not let go hold on,* hold with the
swerving torso rods, insert insert, the puncture wounds were tires on the
weird asphalt her holding on, the distempered body parts will not fail,
the move away like the world collapses when she withdraws her senses,
the absolutely non-existent scenery of the bottom of the water, the world
a fish dark on the bottom and silvery on top, the clouds coming down
swooping down to skim off the refined soils, she was not let go, *hhhh,*
spiritual depth being aligned the whole aspect of the water peeling off
and shouting up into the air, she was not waiting or she had not let go of
her, she would not let go.

[Girl's cartilage feels wobbly]

162

ISLAND

She has to linger at the window whatever the invigilators think. She walks near now looking out, the length of the model table, swings by again heart pounding with absence in the electric blood. She looks near the pool for presence of mind. The building was semi-gilded inside. When the artists finished Girl went hastily outside askew.
Did you want til I'd gone? she asked storming up, the white paint on her head streaked fight for your encounter even if. (The baby was present, tiny as an envelope in the distended belly) Girl the remote. Someone's head was in the water by the air. Tiny bubbles.

It wasn't the same people at all, replacement. The heavy bag at her side with the work papers she could refuse. His papers false labor.

She hadn't waited, no – obeyed the slavery of her sharpened legs, the lights of the communal shone on sideways. *No.* The air bristled as she walked back to the side door fully clothed by these pool-struck people held by rivet talk. That you could be all these experiences and they would be non-evident most of the time, irrelevant to an encounter. That was the first time in the blue dress from the box with her dank hair up, the tea walls. The whole casket of the selfhood folded in. It was totally like completely like. Her opera painting was deep red encased with black on one side, blue, then open canvas. She had been *given in.*

AMBIENT CHAMBER

Girl lay back with her thought patterns swirling, wet dimension voices in the cabinet of her tranquil pockets inside her lively chambers. She *thunked and thunked*, a word she associated with the rough point of her travels. Her caves. She is ambient in filtration, the stiff resistance temporary of the recipient plugs. Without saying anything since today she decides to say nothing for the duration if there's more than one person there. If one

[SHE WEARS A BLUE DRESS MATCHING HER SKIN: EARLIER, IN A MEMORY]

announced oneself as *dumb* people were delighted since you could "speak eye" with them anyway, and they could eye you with impunity as though you were naked or a stranger.

A private limb language might be developed she exteriorized, a canvas body taut as salt on brine filled down.

Walking the way to town meant the cars would go by and each one was someone who was expanded to a two-ton version of itself, breathing the gaseous equation of expansion and weight with a surety of importance as naturalized as it was body-free.

She walks dumbly to town after lying down, the birds occasionally swoop at a distance, their hearts fluttering rapidly against the pressure of their wings, figuring the resistance of the sky-winds pressing them. *Whoosh. Whoosh.* Her voice whirrs locomotive.

POOL
Trees stood hovering nearby her saturated brain, she strokes the bark without meaning to and finds herself beside the stream. Cambium, bark, novitiate, hhhh. She uses her picture tools to adapt a flat sense of sight she's learned out of the water, that bending no longer apparent since she is rounded, the silent air buffering her thick torso. *Stream.*

Every now and then a wind stream reminds her of those times when perfect whooshing brought close sounds and smells of nearby bodily events in the water – darkened energy thinly flatly screeching and hollowing brought to your nerve ears rushes by, so conscious of the sounds and smells seamed together, implicated totally as a current that envelopes and goes by. Then. Here the birds seemed to emanate from a fixed spot outward in a circumspect ring. Ow.

[GIRL CLOSES HER MOUTH AND SWAYS IN HER LABORING BODY]

O wow. *How could she make water art*
Girl thinks it might be fluid something quite different, *a curatorial
headache* surely laughing, yes, a set of features that moved constantly.

And then there would be the upsetting of the humidity quotient of the
Rooms of Art, how tragic, how circumstantial!
Here was something to hover for, stroke stroke, ow, maybe try to make
that happen. Her bristling skin enormous to her touch, blue legs nodding.

Evident art object one: the first one a small deep pool, perfectly oval,
with purified water to demonstrate the blueness of its color against the
white floor of the depth.

He was remonstrating and she saying nothing with her skin nor eyes nor
mouth. Oh let art speak for us with surface depth, let us tickle it without
idea. The next one was a bath of clear blue glue in remonstrance, with
hands. *Where are the hands? Where?*

Maybe action makes the hue, differently from colors not in water, think
of that. She wrote text panels in paint, describing only the materials
and physical principles at work, forbidding the insertions of those pre-
interpretations that withhold. Come along, walk along. The necessity to
paint him.

The shape of Woman and Baby, Ocean and Sky, Ambient. Semi-eternal.
Glued in the salt water. Her muscles firmly grip, hard.

Then the red and action pillows. You couldn't let out much at a time,
reach over and *ow* you're amplitude. *Hhhh.* The canvas of his ideas was
bigger from a distance.

[HER ART RE-EMERGES WATER]

The pain concentrates and her canvas-lined container is like a wooden
bath, something to hold ensuring as she pushes and her firm tight middle
set and push and – everything comes out on it, the saline the bloody
the complete, the little one mooking and sucking for air the twine and
holding her away, the suckling hold the tender one we all could see the
bloody wetness image fabulous on the off-white sampling canvas; and
then after lying quiet being semi-dead attached, and after that again, *ow*
the beautiful organ pushes out smooth and bumpy almost in her mouth
she was hungry no no leave it: everything must be layered and thick
and then preservatives and the laminate thickly appliquéd the title of the
piece Everything But The Baby, no she knew what to call it: *Mother and
Child*.

MY SHAPE YOUR SHAPE
Blood flows between her legs warm and sticky with clots and swirls
afterward. She painted it that way. Her white pants turned pink, loose
as she rinses them. She faces at the passersby who were in on various
secrets they suppress to mend their days.

KINETIC
She is drawn to it, sheets across wet canvas wrapped around soft
cylinders sewn in patterns, a sewing machine configured to inscribe
words as stitch patterns in place of simple hemi-lines. You would have
to bring your eye up close the manual small sewing machine would have
been stitching in the words over and over again
portents on the skin portents on the skin portents on the skin and then re-toggle
like that little machine could be
*a newness all but famished a newness all but famished torn blue torn blue tear that
cocoon and suckle, the dulcet garments cocoon the dulcet blue torn, a newness all
but portents bring up pearls bring up pearls carmine pearls out again re-toggle
they harm and glowing underhead they harm and glowing underhead wink it out*

[GIRL GIVES BIRTH AND MAKES NATAL ART]

wink it overboard abuts the air, a seemly snap abuts the air a seemly comment
mount the snap, the fuzzy head the comment mount so sweat
as apricots hung out to wear on a cloth museum tree inside will bring
you visions.

She makes it like that, a soft blanket that can be wet or dry no matter,
and for the little one. The needle and her blood sewn in, the little holes
for breathing pouring out. She looked, head turning, when she found the
manual sewing machine in an auction house on a wooden table painted
tusk white beside the silver umbrella. The blanket speckles brown and
red and cream and dark and blue.

Now that it was done she sits in an intrepid sheet, stolidly beside her
new bloody show as it's mounted.
The gallery is small and friendly, isolated, with a grocery store down
the street where people could get a bit of food before or after they came
to see. Girl lists to the side above an hour, a hood of planning shadows
imaginatively cast inside her brain while she is thinking. A little cash
would be nice to make the next move.

Do they like it what do you believe? Her friend runs her hands over the
laminate and looks at Girl. She offers to her friend's visiting hands a
sheeted hand and "hello" painted on a small piece of wood to render
solitude immune. *How fey, how mon'aventure, but there you are, we can forgive*:
make room, open up, show art.

Purposive and light later on she stood up and the show had come to an
end for the day. She gathers her little one blanket heaves her breathing
suckling smooth as melted honey glass, sweet one given.

The next valley over was the oceanic cusp she recognizes mostly by
smell, the sharp salty tang, the shifts of air visiting all that monthly

[She makes a biological blanket for her infant]

night could turn to dawn the sky not only blue but also torn. She had never noticed that along the concrete sidewalk hereabouts, the sky blue and torn, the paper bag of salted bread she munched on as she walked, the lingering emoluments of day on her moist skin (she was having a post-serene former walk that time with Ramsey when her legs hurt so much having been carved out for this turn, the dive into a median lake asserting a tangential certitude like definite blue or green). Ramsey of the dead.

Her oranges were peeled and she ate them now. The hour wrinkled in its airdrops as they perspired over her head and in her brain a kindness, remembering that earlier walk as though accumulation was the nature of learning to walk: each time you walk you take every walk you have ever given and the heaviness comes upon you like. Accumulated trajectories. Nibbling on this little rock is like that, to get more salt, mix it with bread and oranges, paste the green, feed the little sharp soft mouth.
And tired dust he lit the candles beside the table later, they just collapsed.
A court of wreckage takes you by the dangling fingers, he explained, with a concomitantly languished intensity, as though extending his own hand outward were a reflection of the times when he had done so whether in seemly or unseemly circumstance.

She likes his causal clothes, their linkage to his work his absent patience. He wore the same thing all the time except late at night when he reduced himself to pale undergarments, the characteristic expressive minimal protection of a young cultural definition.

Come clean, tell me your whole story, don't hold anything back, make like the world can give you a moment of absolute transparency and absolute fullness at once where nothing's missing make it up to me and simultaneously climb on me and yield your pillaged bottom so I can enter you with a massive commonality that makes you stand for everything I want.

[GIRL FEEDS THE INFANT TINY MASHED PROTEINS. BI-FEEDING SHE THINKS WITH THE MOUTH]

She understands that like the clicks and keens and wails.

But to do that you would have to be inside my mirroring, to be consequential without cease; that would suppress every element of backache on the waves. The ship would fall and the argument, the parallel. Her hand's upon the blanket of her child.

The bread and oranges were delicious, they are gone. She walks with the paper bag held carefully in her other hand.

THE CONVERSATION
In the area I was describing pieces of language that become convincing, that show her with feet like knives and her raspy tongue, she opens her eyes to wet encumbrance. She arrives without importance to be liked, although she lives the spleen of love betwixt excessive persons. No matter the danger of pronouns, I am like one is a mirror for the other we. *Picking this up from the frayed mimicry of the intense respect I bear, the wayside greens yield up a spearmint, biting into the delicate edges of the tongue.*

She replies in her amphibious mind, like placing your hand flat, once, distinctly, on a large rectangular table full of water, which absorbs the motion of your hand and spreads responsively. Moving her hand across the water. "I have enjoyed myself tremendously."

He demurred, not that I have any particular aversion to explanation but the appropriate image is never transferred to the appropriate room when you are talking, this imaginary filled-in tank of tabled water is like a parcel that has no address.
She has a wary approach to usefulness and she rectangulates her mouth.
He opens another bottle. They have *another lovely evening* and the baby's real.

[HER BED-SHEETS ARE LIKE THE PAGES OF WAVES]

EURYBATHIC
And euryhaline she is, hence her adaptable approach, she is deep in and over her head, she is satisfied and reprobate, she is tiny against the scope of silty water and enormous in the tub.

Her emergence lo these seasons ago *(as long as we've been together)* was marked by a slow transparency lifted up like an invisible dress, a slight shrieking in the ears and a surface over her eyes that took some time to turn into another basal film, as if the ocean were inside her brain and slowly trickling out through her eyes, imperceptible but for when the wind stirs them up or sweating. People here *noticed*, they were close enough, they are glued, sympathetic and supine in the face of non-understanding. Girl instood the visitation, she is peeling. Walking almost letting go. Which doors and windows are open in your body and which do you imagine no one sees.

[HAVING GIVEN BIRTH, GIRL'S LAND SKIN PEELS]

THIRTEEN
[BLEEDING]

SHE WALKS AT NIGHT
Girl stands on a hill near the entrance to the sea and contemplates
mercury mind, that pool wet line along the twitch of the sky-meets-sea
out there, eyes up eyes down. The pools like clouds like pulsing blood
surges inside her brain the legs twitch. Ay ay ay.

Toward the hemisphere is a blue syringe, her needle eye pucked up to
that direction. The rocks and dirt and insect vegetation are soft beneath
her spiked held standing. She'd kept on cutting her hair for brushes.
She's sewn some in the blanket. The bolted attractions of main worlds,
the incredible loud sighs like the slow beating of atmospheric peristalsis,
hhhh, ssss, hhhh, sea she didn't breathe.
Was every rustle something breathing she wonders?
Every rustle was something breathing all right.
The dawn is a blue prepuce fondling its edges. Walk step breath, walk
step breath, walk step breath, walk step breath. The air is pellucid, sure
of itself, the air is visible enough to allow her outline to propel in front of
her, her head singing and dancing inside with continuity opaque, *I mean
it is shrilly whistling with a high-pitched hum pulse, it's throbbing with tin, it's
replete with a piercing onomatopoeia* the occasional bird sound fed in echo.

Walk, step, breath. The hillside rumbled with experience, the town is

[THE OTHER SHORE AT LAST]

171

without edges has no borders simply vanishes at this edge and at another, it spills out in a last heave of one house then nothing.

The people in these houses were invincible, they have salt and pillows and each other, their lives entire devotion to the tight-knit shared attention. They smile with their muscles and grimace with media semaphores, their hair all up or down, their hand waving and teeth. They are both and neither here nor there, though *here* feels to them like acquisition – or like nothing until someone *change the furnishings or call me.*

Pink socks, blue babies. A balance, a perch of feet on company.
Walk step breath, walk step breath.
The offspring wrapt against her. Her head is balanced on her shoulders with effort, the muscles and tendons microscopically collapsing, the green stuff of the hillside now more pale, the scent of sage and soft waft puffing near her face as she lay down her blanket wet cohabiting. It's a warm night, the end of an artistic day.

The decision she could make was going or not going which was coming or staying or returning, it was – everything else felt handed around her, slow motion speeded up diagonally across aerated courses among faces, greeting, wanting, learning, the blanket and the sweet little heavy animal. And she is after it all by the sea. Which border should she turn now for her aggregate animal?

The light makes her body more and more real to herself on the ground, the body touched by the hands of the borrowed friend whose desuetude imbalanced her; then they both balanced, the searching for the holes of the body and finding them and fitting things inside.
There is time then for the Rooms of Art. She opens her mouth and holds on for weeks, ama, her body reintact.

[AT NIGHT THE GROUND RELEASES DAY-HELD LIGHT]

Couple couple. Her body has holes for breathing and fingers could find them and everything have a hold: fingers, tongue, knees, genital protrusions holding the sides for breathing, and the mouth and torso and vagina.

Couple couple. The sanctimony of the loose rectangle, the damp extrusions. Walk step breath, walk step breath. *Joy of desiring* fitting out the air to a rapturous echo, water to sky. Emptying out the premises. If you are art you can turn yourself inside, out. The town had come to its end.

Coloring

Below, she is a cleft in time, the red gobs plopping from her vaginal innards into the toilet bowl, falling heavily the size of plums, figs, rosettes, red skin almond droppings, the intense sheen of the water heaving carmine red, gypsy red, the droplets like a canvas marking red up to the sides, her hands covered with red, the goblets on the paper – taking them over to the art room by the canvas, painting them, painting with them, what will it do to the consistency? She has on her black underwear nothing else, the shades up high on the upper floor and no one to see. She is walking back to the toilet room every half an hour, the giblets shooking out of her and down. She has a sizable collection the paint is beginning not to sit the same way on the sliding canvas that she tilted backward to hold it still she would caution it with shellac she would mortalize the damned thing.

What are the names in the solid soft pliant figs of gentle red siding made inside her? Artery vein submission, priapus resilience, clandestine modeling of the naked self in front of the mirror to be the model she couldn't afford, the sloping down of the back water, condemnation, holding up her head the black squares of the netting over the mirror to give perspective a catchment, the net her offspring fell through – estuary ovarian, drainage fluid all around the air seeping into her and out, the little holes for breathing *hhhhh*, fallible and open. The canvas as the organ

[Girl makes menstrual art]

173

she grows: she picks up the phone she calls her friend come over and see no give me a minute, give me half an hour, it's raining again the dull ground hopes. Clandestine, the brush clotting on the mat, you bury the remains gently under the tree where you can see them when you leave and then return, re-loop, return. You want to touch another with your process, deliquescent smear.

Conversation

See how that line is streaking across the medial arrangement you have set up with the recessed paint?

Yes, yes I think I do.

Well you need to move that line because it is distracting to the viewer who prepares himself for a particular journey across the board.

Oh ok.

You see you need to move that line because you have simulated a set-up that is to the advantage of the interloper, the one entering from the left because of course that is the direction we go in western art you have read that in your studies –

Yes.

Good well see how the line moves in three directions simultaneously at this point and it isn't a goddamn palm we're looking at I mean you are not a soothsayer right? Right well we could debate that – so the line that is uppermost has the quotient of sensate judgment, that one, there, in the middle has a kind of journey quality and the bottom one, the bottom one there it's the one we associate with not quite knowing what the work is up to, right?

[The art teacher responds to Girl's painting]

I guess you could say that, you could see it that way.

So then this is the line, this one here, that you need to make the thickest one, the one that posits the dominant strain of the work, because the viewer – they're going to be back about here, right?, and they are going to need to know which line is the most important one to follow with their eyes – you'll often see that in the movement of spectators' bodies at the openings, you know, the way it takes almost a consistent amount of time for them to cross the visual field of a particular work, well they are looking for the dominant line and here, right here, is your chance.

Ah, ah.

BUT IN THE MORNING NO
The filling sounds infuse-disperse the air, not deep-through like the water, wake up, keep moving your torso plangent – the sound stops and starts, it's the sound of la vita nuova struggling in her cloths. The vita nuova is hungry from your body, for your ears, your holding smell. She's stronger and tenser now her breathing wet and dry, wet and dry in turns. You hold her raspy gentle skin its bifurcates.

No good can come of it, no creeping across the floor in the middle of the night hoping the light doesn't hit you, no crawling up to the casement to check out what is in the outer street, as though the streetlight would illuminate those boxes on the corner and render them heavenly, escapist. The rungs of the ladder attached to the playground equipment at the school yard down the street, what is that? The rungs that reach up much higher than little people can climb. The rungs on the window that reach outward across the panes of glass. Why the night-time and the day is something to which she never has answer, coming up to being-meaning surfeit, okay that fits the arc of undersea that belly, plop drop there.

[HER DAUGHTER-BABY THICKENS]

175

Girl sits by the edge of the window while the other sleeps. Blood art. Nothing in her hands but the air she is sifting back and forth, the winds slight from the casement. The conversation didn't "get" anywhere so much as forward the hesitations of the set piece, that is delineate how this was going to be like one version of a mini-tale and not another, score another type, not dirty mentoring as before, not so many *accurate* conversations.

It is temperate here by the window, the damp attitude in her veins being something she could recognize even without a hint. Undulate. Keep moving. All the scales work together to achieve a harmony that is like no sound at all. Constative baby, grow and be with me, be with me not with me not me.

Fish
Holding her is like a soft damp cushion aligned against the body, warm with unexpected rivulets, a folding into curves one didn't realize before. Her lips are warm and compressed, her young eyes opening into rivulets, hair shuffled outwards with lively impression as she musters in her mouth.

Because the change in circumstance – because you can swim through the ocean entirely without cease without a block inside – the apartment, the street, turns into a drama set. It all turns into a harbor, a fancy room, the distances not the same as when you walked them earlier, the appearance of others irrelevant, the light slow. The building of expectations is beside them both in its red swarm, the modeled bestiaries the smiles. What you want for your own directives and what worlds offer for anyone. Her breasts are warm pulses, fluid, her body aches the wrong direction inward, re-settling.

[Girl feeds her shedding body-skin to her daughter]

When your body becomes a world and you swim in its arranged reflection of a known world does it combine. Microchasm.

Wet threads beneath her and outward, argyle stones below and the clatter of pine needles against her ear; she is pattern resting, blowing the wet air across her little holes for breathing. She has been stretched out under that tree for many hours, the argyle stones were softly pressed into the earth and the pine needles made it ok. Then their pattering woke her ears.

EVENT HORIZON

The light was gentle through the edges of the tree and she knew outside the tree was morning, near the edge of the tribal area where the weaving work was languishing, the cooking languishing. Except that the weaving work itself was brought presumably by the aspects of the material land and the pottery had risen up from the ground whose stones had been separated out and were like babies, the earth mulch giving.

Girl no longer inquires what it means to absorb the questions, to provide the needed water. I mean would you. Just get the information nearby. Something happens and something else happens and it's supposed to be all right.

Girl walks over to the kind-looking persons by their truck and they give her water, she kisses their little child. All morning long her body stretches out as she plays with the little child near the truck by the side of the road where her mother sells bags and beads, she and the child having little to say to each other but much to explore in the stones and lack of water. Animals take the rocks up and provide them.

That morning by the pines erased her questions, the little one gentle nudging. Further on she will find more water, but this absence of speaking is what she needs.

Pouring in to that silence.

[CAN SHE AND SHE BECOME LAND ANIMALS?]

At the shop she reads the newspaper. What are normal dots; but certainly the banning of words is no surprise, not having heard collapsed available language freely aired in this converted passage.

Where on earth are the barnacles? Where are the putrid stamina modes, the wafting elements thick with the devoured leftovers of a meal that took place back on inner waves long back?

The leftover calm resorts. A pattern of a story, a briefer patter, the talkback employment. Every event happens and remains happening.

Everything settles gently to a plateau now much more fertile in blood. Every time she sits on the toilet more small pieces of her drop out in warm red clumps, globules of meaning excluded, inner and outer skins. Her flesh resumes its outlines when she stands, but where is the pressure to hold her? The sea to hold her tight its swaddling tense. That press defines large calm.

Back at the store where she picks up her friend she studies the message on the screen, *the service is powered for more information* proactive anti-viral (the tiny claws on the buds of the eyelashes look) around the globe, visit advertised practice an *unincorporated association standards authority* like one-two, heave-ho the one that different artist (Georges de la Tour). She imagines responding to the possibility of retribution for the insult of mortality – not with my own hand would I take up arms, but neither would I stop anyone doing so – *registered office mid city*, stay on the right side of the up-to-database advice. Girl could imagine multiple warring approaches to be the thrust of anger at the insult of succession now directed to the other, who would *take it* which how could they not – the rise of the global spreading across the identity patterns of people's faces so they'll drop their names? The pattern of interactive species haulage? Give up your name and something else will hold you. The deep erase.

[What does the land world connect within itself?]

Her friend smiles, having to take off the skin of that day to emerge into an alternate non-economic reality they have talked about, relations not being predicated on a module of exchange except that they eat together and have rested together and given each other, thereby, orts and companionship and arguably co-sustain one another's dimensions, as though they were the water pressure she misses in a negative sense, *I mean does her body remember as a mode of experience,* the tension holding the replete accumulations of the events all round them, those having to become microscopic variables of which their chemical agencies were aware but which they themselves, needing the settled-down air and light, kept their heads above while walking back to the apartment.

It was something like tragedy, she read. Like a mistaken identity wedged next to an unassumed one. Even there, bottomless, you can stay next to each other until death rise from within or from without.

Her head aches with undirected clemency. Because talk is a placement patch for other talk, a kind of visible armory replacement – she can see that, she has learned it like new turns she learned and "grew." Flicking your appendages, rolling your head at the right time. That head has been *scanned for power telomeres,* needing a proactive round visit, associated with self-giving as when you're sitting here incorporated with the hand of Standard Authority.

LOCAL KNOWLEDGE
In the morning her friend said
come with me to the bus stop at the station mid town, stay on the right side of the database, I'll tell you straight, make sure you are free and relevant help, make sure you are available on the site. *You're allowed to want what you want.* What have you got to lose?

[GIRL PUSHES BACK HER LAST LAND LOVE]

What's missing? *We have used the information you have given us,* we have turned it frequently two directions (together with other information from or about you) to set up two possibilities, the escape artist and the devotionist, to take compliance, push in and out, believe and in non-believing make a route.

Her friend was a woman with a ready heart. *We may contact you with escape opportunities at whatever point; we may show you new devotion events and opportunities; we may contact you or give you our activities, come let us know.*

Her friend took her art *in the best possible sense.* An anti-viral regulator has the system in its sites – whatever is left over – what's the structure of experience once the body's been taken out, element father, element mother, broken edges furrowing through, the face looking up at you from the water's edge, the tethers and opportunities within the little holes for breathing *hhhhhhh.*

[Girl gets on the bus]

FOURTEEN
[SPRUNG]

VERNAL POOLS

Bait and switch, the salamander as delicious as pod pies, the offspring tiny droplets in the water as though she were peeing there from above. She had left the sassy person's computer by the water line and it had dropped in, as though she'd planned it that way. It was a present of consciousness in any event: though she would miss it, she would not miss its attachments. There is the matter of language, her eyes getting really tired from the reading, what it meant to divest. Almost every Presbyterian family within fifty miles had given that community a sharebreak, defined as giving back what someone was going to give you later once you had received it in your time of need. Or something near. She works to stand the pleasantries. "Oh say it sure has been nice having you working up at the paper store there." Why. Why has it been nice to say. But there's slippage for you, geographically instanced separation zones among skin touters. It's dreamy in the water near, where their bodies glimmed and gathered. The salamanders carried the moisture everywhere, on the rocks in her mouth, on the little holes for breathing pulsing out.

BLOODY SHOW

The tender os cried irretrievable. Her eye opened and the baby came out. While her legs were spread she could see the far side of the horizon

[GIRL RIDES THE BUS TO THE FERRY LANDING, REVISITING PRIOR EVENTS WITH HERETOFORE UNREVEALED SENSATIONS]

manually, her arms peripheral and spread. Place that in the order of events.

Her black line came on fast, like the sideline ache on each side of her body had always been there she felt – when people passed by in the darkness with her sides always near, as though she exists in outline, for outside the water now her central line would be contractual black.

In the time of the breaking of waters, they come out like she has from the ruptured recall of her maternal, of the ocean waving in terrestrial animosity but completing, licking against the damp and dry sides of the encrusted earth, the baby that squalled in the winds that came forth from her timely ejaculations, her contractual dependency, why hadn't she asked anyone to come with her (she would eat them they would come too close) there was no-one there the canvas in her teeth damp compressed. Her very thick torso squeezed red and blue. The shore breaks over the rocks, sand, grasses, breakwater, bridges, swelling the bay, surging the lines of roads and roads, standing up in your houses.

She coos, she forms air. She licked the vernix from the baby's skin, it is like the damp on cheese she spat out from the grocery store her very nice friend had brought her; but the skin was perfect. Girl licked her lips and the warm smears were like some fathomable gloss, and in her mouth it was a real live coating, it sank slowly down her throat it was like the thick packed breast the baby would vacuum with a tight suction seal against her skin she hadn't planned on feeling, feeding.

Fertilization culture would decree the line beside paternity blank, someone would write "unknown" above the causeway after she squeezed the child from her liquid encampment. But the extension outward and bringing back inside, it was like self-travel in concert with the efforts of

[GIRL RE-EXPERIENCES "GIVING" BIRTH. SPLIT OPEN THE BODY RELINEATES]

all others touching you. Her torso shapes back in the muscles: that clenches good. *Mother and Child* came out well; that piece presents its laminate witness every time she smiles when she thinks of that.

Yum yum but she couldn't eat the baby, its skin was furry went all the way through its body. Tender pie. The warm damp blanket sewn for holding her. Girl licks her arm and holding, *hhhh*, breath.

BIOMORPH
One animal goes into one body and another one comes out, the flesh folds back and forth in a friended change.
Inside the sea the worlds were day-night, slow hovering and flexing vertical borders, magnetic emoluments enticing.
Here on ground our day comes through as one specific site we walk gentle to each other, as though behindhand, born with the morning we encircle. Exchanging parts. Or like a layering effect one atop or one beside the other, floating. *You don't come back to you.*
She tells the baby about these differences, passing her magnetically over land, over water, on land, inside the water.

People play music to distract their consequences, to set a feeling, to take over the air with culture, to stimulate a quiescent background sense imbued. It is very exciting walking amidst them. Girl notices their nerves respond, how much their skin is thrilled, inveigled, soothed, stimulus. They poach each other, they simmer and roil, they are delicious in the sun with the salt extruding as though getting ready to eat themselves, they sit in the afternoon alcove and eat and lick their own fingers delicious. The children in the avenues stinking of their bodies and dirt and delicious, kind of sour and earth with a deep coat of sugar involved. Girl walks amidst them thrilling, the tongues of her inner skin

[THINKING AS NERVE MOUTH]

licking in imagination every coat of skin hovering near. They are lavish and gathered in parks and walkways. All of us imagining we are alone. Imagine!

The park hovers near its design, stroking it thoughtfully. If there were more trees or conversely if a desert had been put deliberately amidst this avenue, what kinds of animals might come? What kinds of underground insects and polymorphs?

When the rain hits the park people come running because of the ingenious scents tucked into the greenery waiting. In the springtime groups of people come to play sports and dig pegs into the ground. The park remembers those pegs, it is full of seams and rivulets that keep the moles and mammals company, that send them rivulets.

DAPHNE
Girl sat under the tree. Nearby the park a building has its own diagonals, longing to cross the river and be near the pink cocoon of the skating rink, to keep it company. The building is deprived of agency only by the minds of its observers: *look look* says another. People came and covered the building in waste, Girl smelled and saw it. It was in the newspapers. For months, nothing, then emerged in a pattern of syllables across and down each slab. Aquarium. *Look look*. A building sent to waste, geography as an extension of your mind, a play set on the edge of a welcoming precipice.

That night Girl visited taking her tongue across the building to taste the new design you remember. Crystalline parameters and cool willingness, the building thrilled to her. She took a whole image of the building and put it in her mind to take out later for fondling. Mmmm.

[WITH AGENTIVE BODIES]

She ate the map, the paper clumping in her mouth since she couldn't go back. The food you take as oiled paper saturate with fishes, sweet one, sweet little one, munch and suck.

She heaves out the baby in a tideline that's always here since everything happens constantly once she comes in to the possession of language. *Though her pores heave liquid and her blood moves, her parts slip comfortable wet, fall out, retain their present shape within.* The wind is like a margin in the air, pepper spray ameliorated seasoning in the air, *I don't know* comparatives.

This place however *knows* itself, as in self-devouring the repeated patterns of changing industry and the constant low-level hum of surprise, cloistered so long as the walls are held loosely enough, "gotcha" patents with or without sympathy.

Girl builds a sandy fountain: she pees in the park at night. Hunkered down over her skirt, ready for action.

RECUR
Oh I see, the event moves and you can see it. It doesn't stop moving. The friend had been suddenly dying, was dying and close by, Girl went to visit, she brought the baby inside, she stood invisible at the bedside. The bed was wrapped in plastic, the limbs were encased, the air smelled like dynamite.
The man with capsules in his front shirt running down a field, running, the roar of the airplace overhead she was inside it the airplace roared beside the bed they were redeeming themselves with statues it was a time of great unpeeling, the rifle shot – skimmed across the blanket, she held it down again, the drawings showed all that.
As here in the road rise up waves the bus a whale.

[EVENTS WET SHADOWS WIPE RECUR]

185

The nurses were very tired very tired and they yawned they had limbs
stretched toward limbs they stood very high up above the bed the
clinging bed. Girl was nervous her friend could not hear anything they
said, they were mouthing to her friend. Her friend was nervous, she
could not hear anything, the friend thought herself unwielding was not
dying, it was not possible to situate herself where dying was a plane
roaring outside the window of the imagined desert.

FRAME
There in the cool breeze hammering on the moon at night as she walked
(this was earlier) in some trance of saturation knowing the air was being
sucked out of the tiny holes for breathing (this was her friend) having
told her the story of her own passage across the great divide and how the
air sucked all the moisture out of her and she had turned (horror) into
an air shape and magnanimous sang against the full scope of the trip;
this was not a requirement, some people never left at all. They were not
poles they were blanks on fault this angst.

This was the bathroom, just off her room there were flying particles
across her face, there were red splotches temporary, holding, she could
smell the nerves.

Girl came back in the room and bent over her friend and spoke quietly
for some time. She kissed the quiet cheek. The automatic doors closed
and shivered open half-way and then closed.

The room was still for a long time. It sighed. The windows were flat
against the walls they sighed. The windows clearly changed constantly,
they held great interest. The baby sighed up and down in its delivered
life.

[FIVEFOLD ADVENTURES WRITE THEIR PRIVATE HISTORIES]

On the road
The decision is no longer hers only. That's a meaning of the split. You
turn them around and life faces on the other side, neither a triumph of
the will nor its opposite, but the shift makes difference and that makes
– no to leaving the warm ground, sometimes it's lovely, all that walking
turns you into a warm wave on the ground. But there's a place, a place
to – get on the bus. She'd gone back in the hospital room to gather up
the one who's tethered to her now. The exteriorization not of self but a
dialectic that splits off, proving one point of relation.

Girl moves her legs and shifts the small one, more desired, tinier and
denser than you think. From one breast to the other, suckling the
warm wet globe, Girl sees – she has a pineal window. There's the spot.
Microchasm of water sounds, tidal pools surrounded by warm soft
blankets, you can picture it, mirror, mira.

So here they are on the upper deck, no they call it the extension, upper
back part, the layering effect of breathing passages, you walk upward
the people reclining with their spines, they are hunched and splintered to
the side, she can hear the nerves complaining. She heaves back fully to
the back.

Welcome on the bus here we begin again a resonant machine, Girl could
smell the hitchhiker from a long way off before a vehicle flipped over
behind them, a small bus without orders or information on the sides, it
rolled end over end but the highway was busy and no doubt the bus she
was on – *the car before then* – had to get where it was going, the people
watching backward or turning it into a report, it was already a report
moving against an artifice of calamity. Her mind like a car, a vat of
water, a set of actions, closing her eyes laterally, a walk in wet darkness,
holding her warm damp blanket to her warm torso. Those times shunt
parallel to this one. The visible sign of her self-difference *born here.*

[She told her friend for those who never came back]

187

She is crossing the small region in the bus without a pass, without water, she drinks the water from the small sink in the bus bathroom that roars and roars, she is gigantic in the bathroom standing there, all the muscles in her face relaxed. She told her the story *you leave to arrive*, she told the story of when she was trapped in an idea of air, never being the return system to water, she is making sounds out loud but not all the sounds were like speaking.

No need to be shy as she listens for the person standing breathing outside the door of the bus bathroom. She is breathing there with the water running on her skin, hhhhh.

Her breathing, her libido, the waves, her breathing *hhhh* the rooms, cars, opening out, a gentle entropy of pattern noise, salt fixes and damp marrow dirt, the daughter in the crevice sea by the tender rocks, her snout pressed gently to the roseate path of chemicals, amphibious traduced. That's the opening, that's her name: *Mira*.

[GIRL CHRISTENS HER DAUGHTER ON THE BUS]

188

POSTLUDE

REAR WINDOW
The bus has a behind, she is placated. She pushes back against the back
of the bus and has a behind. Her buttocks soft and resonant in pants,
the seat flat against her legs the back of the bus square and the window
behind announcing the ongoing stratosphere, her friends in both
replete. She held her hand in the moving room gently disappearing, the
outer layer peeling off imperceptibly scatter. Baby of mine, your body
announces you. That holding saturates the present that she misses, very
dear.

FERRY
Come soon, come back soon!
The woman played in the room that night seeking pranks, the wind
pushing its "agenda" like the man said back then in the fulsome
abbreviations of partnership. He said over and over, the faces turned
toward each other smelling, eyeing, discovering, turning the body.
She holds her back to the pictures and smells them with the skin at her
back, they were animated and moving. The people were tenuous, the air
holding them unconscious of it, they fled themselves continually, because
to look at the thing in front being countenanced is a demographic of –
the body cannot swallow.

[A REAL BUS]

189

From the bus, they take the ferry over earlier that day, Girl and her girl lingering, the water moving like land pushes sometimes, like land moves much more slowly, you move along and it hums too, the magma deep under ground answering the thick skin at the top, adamant silty trope vibrating no blanks at all.

Look at that vista lookit over here!
Every person full of her own familiar, transient familiar, breathing in and out familiar. In every comportment home her skin electric continual, the tendrils pushing out.

Initially she pushes her limbs softly into earth to get the sense of minerals. This incredibly soft tongue of nursing, the skin going all the way through her dense sand yielding to inner swirl, the savory water rushing in. Copious drag and succulent machinery of the place!
There had been a chance, a soft pad tender rivulet to leave a daughter whose life – but here she could breathe, she could breathe in the sea.

Gentle gentle, come'st thou back to me, my true blood gainful as a purge, if you will one's darling one given to sacramental heave one and one very much renewing sever, not to you let go not to let you go.
She is a regenerate organ, this one, giving the sea body to sea body turning inside out unpeeling cumber. The turn like sweetest eviscerate, nearer to hap and come along. It's a way of talking to someone who has no set departure, who represents the rebirth of unknowing.

Girl sinks her lips against her arm to lick the sweat, swirling her tongue a little bread in her mouth the moisture tang. It's a better way to smell than obedient distance. She'd often lain up on the ground to sweat. In bed at night the seaweed rank damp sheets, flapping you wet swirl, the window pane very near wet with previous rain.

[A REAL FERRY]

Very pregnant with ideas she is on the boat going to the island part, she is passing the monkey stuck together, monkey it was Hear No Evil, See No Evil, Speak No Evil welded together in burnt wood ash. It recognizes her as she passes on the island line, the quay held itself out as far as possible to reach her, she is torrential in her mind with the sea up against the other side of the main door to her cloistered identity, awa pushed-up part seen clear.

The woman who was leading the way proper with a retrograde compliance was a herder, the several figures. You move the ways your atmosphere permits. You can walk this path to the beach or I can lead you, *we're here for two hours then the boat goes back.*

Really my love. The bird's head went up and down the clarity of open sand, pucked foamy lines by the water. The sand is an enormous cleaned-out funerary beautiful of ground fine tiny-fine bones.

TURN
She hears the several figures gather around their damp electric sightful breathlessness. They are liking a look, they move their mouths, *Look, look!*

Leaning on her lines, the blanket falling tenderly her hands reach by the rushes. The sea is soft and clement, mild and perishable, the sound of air all over her *shhhh, hhhhh, sheeehh*. They could walk apart to turn inside, "all over the island" if they wished. Girl walks apart.

Soft and hush, soft hush, little one come along be all right move your way, *mmmm,* the spracky wash shush shush voice under voice. The wettened sand a soft pad, a pad of rivulets, pretty rocks adventure near.

[AN ISLAND]

191

Girl smiles, the waves break crust, the air gets all penumbral wet legs curl in the sand bones splashing patter. Ahhh, an earth suffused with perfect self-consumption, recycled wishes warmer in the fore-beach, hhhhh, afternoon.

Crest, cusp, solemn depth sediment brushing wet and warm and cool, swirl here on the ambient anatomy, legs arms swirl. You dandle your leg frames open, your head sees the frame of the world is smiling here, hungry and smiling her blue arms, her opening flesh cloak. *Ready, turn again unbend, come along wriggle open your pores.* The lines curve tipple tipple shush, tipple tipple shush, turn with me open your skin now warm this way, now softly dip, breel cusper shoom hmm ahhhm ahhmmmmm. Louder, fuller, open your skin the epicurls, shooom hmmmm down totally in the world you smell remember – wahh awa hmmm zhoooum, move thistle wave a darling sheer in *look*, there you are, closer move out thicker flick as holding, hold full swallow *zzhheeee* here inner wave down swallow, here we swallow, become the see the whirl deep beside you bring yourself together, dun full shaft azora sheem traduction, seam a packer out flick flick – now there, there you are, your thick sharp velvet pushed out smelling the funnel cooler stream out here you're totally incarnate plete out tanser, thoroughly kinetic swirls of sound shock feeling arrow body muscles all together take it fully – us we ripple, ripple arrow blue through the feeling, ama flicker darling ripple with me we already know all pores an open listening move in here through hshh husshhh, ahhmmmm

[Biomorph]

Lisa Samuels is the author of eleven poetry books, an experimental memoir (*Anti M*), and many essays and literary editing projects. Her vocal and instrumental art includes work with composer Frédéric Pattar and a CD version of her book *Tomorrowland*, now being made into a film by director Wes Tank. She has a University of Virginia Ph.D. in poetry and critical practice, and she writes about transculturalism, the body, the ethics of identity, and imagining what we don't know. Born in Boston, Lisa has lived in North America, Europe, the Middle East, and recently Australasia, where she lives in Aotearoa/New Zealand with her partner and son. *Tender Girl* is her first novel.

Lightning Source UK Ltd.
Milton Keynes UK
UKOW04f0721031117

312085UK00002B/174/P